Daily Blood Sugar and Blood Pressure Journal
6-Month Health Monitoring

Name :

Age :   **Gender :**

Address :

Contact information :

INTRODUCTION

Welcome to Your Health Monitoring Journal

Tracking Blood Sugar and Blood Pressure for Better Health

Purpose of the Journal

This journal is designed to help you monitor your daily blood sugar and blood pressure levels. Regular tracking can provide valuable insights into your health, help you manage chronic conditions, and assist your healthcare provider in making informed decisions about your care.

How to Use This Journal

Daily Entries : Each day, you will record your blood sugar and blood pressure levels at different times. This journal provides sections for morning (fasting), before and after lunch, evening, and before bed readings. You can also note your heart rate, medications taken, and any relevant observations.

Weekly Summaries: At the end of each week, use the summary pages to reflect on your readings, note any trends, and set goals for the upcoming week. This helps in identifying patterns and making necessary adjustments to your lifestyle or treatment plan.

Monthly Summaries: Monthly summaries provide a broader overview of your health trends. Reflect on your progress, discuss any concerns with your healthcare provider, and adjust your goals accordingly.

Tips for Accurate Measurements

1. Wash your hands before testing.	1. Sit quietly for 5 minutes before measuring.
2. Use a fresh lancet for each test.	2. Use a properly calibrated and validated monitor.
3. Follow your meter's instructions for proper use.	3. Place the cuff on a bare arm, level with your heart.
4. Record the reading immediately to avoid errors.	4. Take readings at the same times each day

Contact Information :

Healthcare Provider details : [Include your healthcare provider's contact details here]

Emergency Contacts: [List emergency contact numbers here]

1.

2.

"Take care of your body. It's the only place you have to live." — Jim Rohn

HYPERTENSION
What you should know

What Is Hypertension?

Hypertension, or high blood pressure, is a common health problem. Blood pressure is the force of blood pushing against the walls of your arteries as your heart pumps blood through your body. High blood pressure makes your heart work harder with every heartbeat. If you don't get treated for your hypertension, you have a higher risk for heart attack, heart failure, stroke, or kidney failure.

How is Hypertension Diagnosed?

Blood pressure is measured by inflating a cuff around the arm—this is connected to a device that measures pressure. The test is easy and painless. Blood pressure reading is given as two numbers (example: 120/80). The top number is called systolic pressure, and it measures the pressure while your heart is beating. The bottom number is called diastolic pressure and measures the pressure while the heart is relaxed between beats. Ask your doctor what blood pressure reading is normal for you. Adults aged 40years and above must get their blood pressure checked.

What are the symptoms ?

Hypertension often has no symptoms. Sudden adverse events may occur. In patients with hypertension , headache, heaviness in the chest, fatigability may be the presenting symptoms. The only way to know for sure is to take your blood pressure.

✓ **Eat less salt** 

✓ **Lose weight** 

✓ **Exercise** 

✓ **Eat more fruits and Vegetables** 

✓ **Drink less alcohol** 

✓ **Quit smoking** 

✓ **Meditation / Yoga & Relaxation** 

How is Hypertension Treated?

There are many different medicines to help treat high blood pressure. Your doctor may prescribe one medicine or a combination of medicines. Many lifestyle changes can also help to lower your blood pressure. Almost everyone with high blood pressure can bring down their numbers with lifestyle changes, medicines, or both.

 Follow these healthy habits even if you take blood pressure medicine

What is Diabetes?

Diabetes is a condition where there is too much sugar(glucose) in your blood. Sugar can build up because your body doesn't make enough of a hormone called insulin. Diabetes can happen if you don't have enough insulin to turn the sugar into energy. It also may happen if your body doesn't respond to the insulin it does have. Most people with diabetes make at least some insulin, but it doesn't work to keep the blood sugar under control. This is called type 2 diabetes. When type 2 diabetes is not controlled, it can cause sugar to build up. If the sugar stays high, it can slowly damage the heart, kidneys, nerves, eyes, and feet. It is very important to keep type 2 diabetes under control to prevent complications.

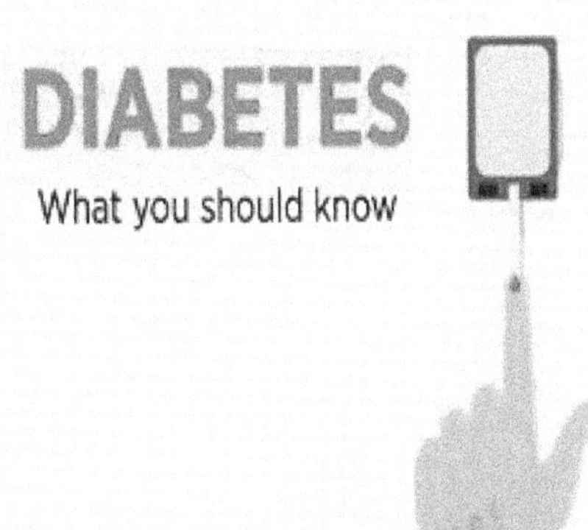

What Are the symptoms/signs of Diabetes?

Symptoms/Signs of diabetes may include:

1. Extreme thirst and/or hunger
2. Fatigue
3. Frequent need to urinate
4. Unusual weight loss
5. Blurred vision
6. Tingling or numbness in hands or feet
7. Frequent infections
8. Bruises that are slow to heal

How is Diabetes Treated?

People with diabetes need to improve sugar (glucose) control in their bodies.

Sometimes, lifestyle changes, such as eating healthy, losing weight, or doing regular exercise, can help improve glucose control. If lifestyle changes don't improve glucose control, your doctor may prescribe medicines.

There are many different types of medicines for type 2 diabetes, including insulin. Not all people with type 2 diabetes will need insulin. Talk to your doctor about what treatment plan is best for you.

How is Diabetes Diagnosed?

Diabetes is diagnosed by testing the level of glucose/sugar, in your blood. Two or more tests might be used to diagnose diabetes. You may need to fast before some diabetes tests. The level of glucose in your blood with overnight fasting is called fasting blood sugar (FBS). Another test is done 2 hours after intake of food – Postprandial Blood sugar (PPBS). When the blood sugar levels are checked at any time of the day, it is called as Random blood Sugar (RBS). HbA1c Test indicates the average glucose levels in your blood over the last 3 months.

Dietary Modifications in Diabetes

Our diet includes three major nutrients: carbohydrates, proteins, and fats. A balanced intake of these nutrients is crucial for maintaining good health, especially for people with diabetes. This is particularly important in southern India, where rice is a staple food.

Key Recommendations:

- Avoid White Rice: White rice has a high carbohydrate content, which can significantly increase blood sugar levels. Consider using grains like oats, barley, quinoa, and other millets instead of white rice.
- Oil Usage: Use oil sparingly. Opt for oils like olive, canola, or peanut oil, which are better for health.
- Vegetable Choices: Replace starchy vegetables like potatoes with green vegetables.
- Dairy: Use fat-free milk to reduce fat intake.
- Condiments: Reduce the consumption of pickles, chutneys, and pappads. For individuals with diabetes and high blood pressure, these should be avoided entirely.
- Hydration: Drink plenty of water throughout the day.
- Food Labels: Always read the nutrition labels on packaged foods to understand their carbohydrate, protein, and fat content.

Date		Day	
Time	Blood sugar (mg/dl)	Blood pressure (mmHg)	Insulin dose/Notes
Morning (Fasting)			
Before Lunch			
After Lunch			
Evening (Before dinner)			
Before Bed (after dinner)			
Midnight			

Date		Day	
Morning (Fasting)			
Before Lunch			
After Lunch			
Evening (Before dinner)			
Before Bed (after dinner)			
Midnight			

Date		Day	
Morning (Fasting)			
Before Lunch			
After Lunch			
Evening (Before dinner)			
Before Bed (after dinner)			
Midnight			

Other information

Date			Day
Time	Blood sugar (mg/dl)	Blood pressure (mmHg)	Insulin dose/Notes
Morning (Fasting)			
Before Lunch			
After Lunch			
Evening (Before dinner)			
Before Bed (after dinner)			
Midnight			

Date			Day
Morning (Fasting)			
Before Lunch			
After Lunch			
Evening (Before dinner)			
Before Bed (after dinner)			
Midnight			

Date			Day
Morning (Fasting)			
Before Lunch			
After Lunch			
Evening (Before dinner)			
Before Bed (after dinner)			
Midnight			

Other information

Date		**Day**	
Time	Blood sugar (mg/dl)	Blood pressure (mmHg)	Insulin dose/Notes
Morning (Fasting)			
Before Lunch			
After Lunch			
Evening (Before dinner)			
Before Bed (after dinner)			
Midnight			

Date		**Day**	
Morning (Fasting)			
Before Lunch			
After Lunch			
Evening (Before dinner)			
Before Bed (after dinner)			
Midnight			

Date		**Day**	
Morning (Fasting)			
Before Lunch			
After Lunch			
Evening (Before dinner)			
Before Bed (after dinner)			
Midnight			

Other information

WEEKLY SUMMARY

Weekly readings Summary

Day	Fasting	Before lunch	After lunch	Evening before dinner	After dinner	Midnight	Blood pressure
Average							

Reflections on diet, exercise, and overall health

Any changes in medication or lifestyle

Goals for the next week

Date		Day	
Time	Blood sugar (mg/dl)	Blood pressure (mmHg)	Insulin dose/Notes
Morning (Fasting)			
Before Lunch			
After Lunch			
Evening (Before dinner)			
Before Bed (after dinner)			
Midnight			

Date		Day	
Morning (Fasting)			
Before Lunch			
After Lunch			
Evening (Before dinner)			
Before Bed (after dinner)			
Midnight			

Date		Day	
Morning (Fasting)			
Before Lunch			
After Lunch			
Evening (Before dinner)			
Before Bed (after dinner)			
Midnight			

Other information

Date		**Day**	
Time	Blood sugar (mg/dl)	Blood pressure (mmHg)	Insulin dose/Notes
Morning (Fasting)			
Before Lunch			
After Lunch			
Evening (Before dinner)			
Before Bed (after dinner)			
Midnight			

Date		**Day**	
Morning (Fasting)			
Before Lunch			
After Lunch			
Evening (Before dinner)			
Before Bed (after dinner)			
Midnight			

Date		**Day**	
Morning (Fasting)			
Before Lunch			
After Lunch			
Evening (Before dinner)			
Before Bed (after dinner)			
Midnight			

Other information

Date		**Day**	
Time	Blood sugar (mg/dl)	Blood pressure (mmHg)	Insulin dose/Notes
Morning (Fasting)			
Before Lunch			
After Lunch			
Evening (Before dinner)			
Before Bed (after dinner)			
Midnight			

Date		**Day**	
Morning (Fasting)			
Before Lunch			
After Lunch			
Evening (Before dinner)			
Before Bed (after dinner)			
Midnight			

Date		**Day**	
Morning (Fasting)			
Before Lunch			
After Lunch			
Evening (Before dinner)			
Before Bed (after dinner)			
Midnight			

Other information

WEEKLY SUMMARY

Weekly readings Summary

Day	Fasting	Before lunch	After lunch	Evening before dinner	After dinner	Midnight	Blood pressure
Average							

Reflections on diet, exercise, and overall health

Any changes in medication or lifestyle

Goals for the next week

Date			Day
Time	Blood sugar (mg/dl)	Blood pressure (mmHg)	Insulin dose/Notes
Morning (Fasting)			
Before Lunch			
After Lunch			
Evening (Before dinner)			
Before Bed (after dinner)			
Midnight			

Date			Day
Morning (Fasting)			
Before Lunch			
After Lunch			
Evening (Before dinner)			
Before Bed (after dinner)			
Midnight			

Date			Day
Morning (Fasting)			
Before Lunch			
After Lunch			
Evening (Before dinner)			
Before Bed (after dinner)			
Midnight			

Other information

Date		Day	
Time	Blood sugar (mg/dl)	Blood pressure (mmHg)	Insulin dose/Notes
Morning (Fasting)			
Before Lunch			
After Lunch			
Evening (Before dinner)			
Before Bed (after dinner)			
Midnight			

Date		Day	
Morning (Fasting)			
Before Lunch			
After Lunch			
Evening (Before dinner)			
Before Bed (after dinner)			
Midnight			

Date		Day	
Morning (Fasting)			
Before Lunch			
After Lunch			
Evening (Before dinner)			
Before Bed (after dinner)			
Midnight			

Other information

Date		Day	
Time	**Blood sugar (mg/dl)**	**Blood pressure (mmHg)**	**Insulin dose/Notes**
Morning (Fasting)			
Before Lunch			
After Lunch			
Evening (Before dinner)			
Before Bed (after dinner)			
Midnight			

Date		Day	
Morning (Fasting)			
Before Lunch			
After Lunch			
Evening (Before dinner)			
Before Bed (after dinner)			
Midnight			

Date		Day	
Morning (Fasting)			
Before Lunch			
After Lunch			
Evening (Before dinner)			
Before Bed (after dinner)			
Midnight			

Other information

WEEKLY SUMMARY

Weekly readings Summary

Day	Fasting	Before lunch	After lunch	Evening before dinner	After dinner	Midnight	Blood pressure
Average							

Reflections on diet, exercise, and overall health

Any changes in medication or lifestyle

Goals for the next week

Date			Day
Time	Blood sugar (mg/dl)	Blood pressure (mmHg)	Insulin dose/Notes
Morning (Fasting)			
Before Lunch			
After Lunch			
Evening (Before dinner)			
Before Bed (after dinner)			
Midnight			

Date			Day
Morning (Fasting)			
Before Lunch			
After Lunch			
Evening (Before dinner)			
Before Bed (after dinner)			
Midnight			

Date			Day
Morning (Fasting)			
Before Lunch			
After Lunch			
Evening (Before dinner)			
Before Bed (after dinner)			
Midnight			

Other information

Date			Day
Time	Blood sugar (mg/dl)	Blood pressure (mmHg)	Insulin dose/Notes
Morning (Fasting)			
Before Lunch			
After Lunch			
Evening (Before dinner)			
Before Bed (after dinner)			
Midnight			

Date			Day
Morning (Fasting)			
Before Lunch			
After Lunch			
Evening (Before dinner)			
Before Bed (after dinner)			
Midnight			

Date			Day
Morning (Fasting)			
Before Lunch			
After Lunch			
Evening (Before dinner)			
Before Bed (after dinner)			
Midnight			

Other information

Date		Day	
Time	Blood sugar (mg/dl)	Blood pressure (mmHg)	Insulin dose/Notes
Morning (Fasting)			
Before Lunch			
After Lunch			
Evening (Before dinner)			
Before Bed (after dinner)			
Midnight			

Date		Day	
Morning (Fasting)			
Before Lunch			
After Lunch			
Evening (Before dinner)			
Before Bed (after dinner)			
Midnight			

Date		Day	
Morning (Fasting)			
Before Lunch			
After Lunch			
Evening (Before dinner)			
Before Bed (after dinner)			
Midnight			

Other information

WEEKLY SUMMARY

Weekly readings Summary

Day	Fasting	Before lunch	After lunch	Evening before dinner	After dinner	Midnight	Blood pressure
Average							

Reflections on diet, exercise, and overall health

Any changes in medication or lifestyle

Goals for the next week

MONTHLY SUMMARY

GRAPH SHOWING MONTHLY _________________ (FASTING/PRANDIAL) BLOOD GLUCOSE LEVEL TREND

Plot your blood glucose values on the graph and join the points

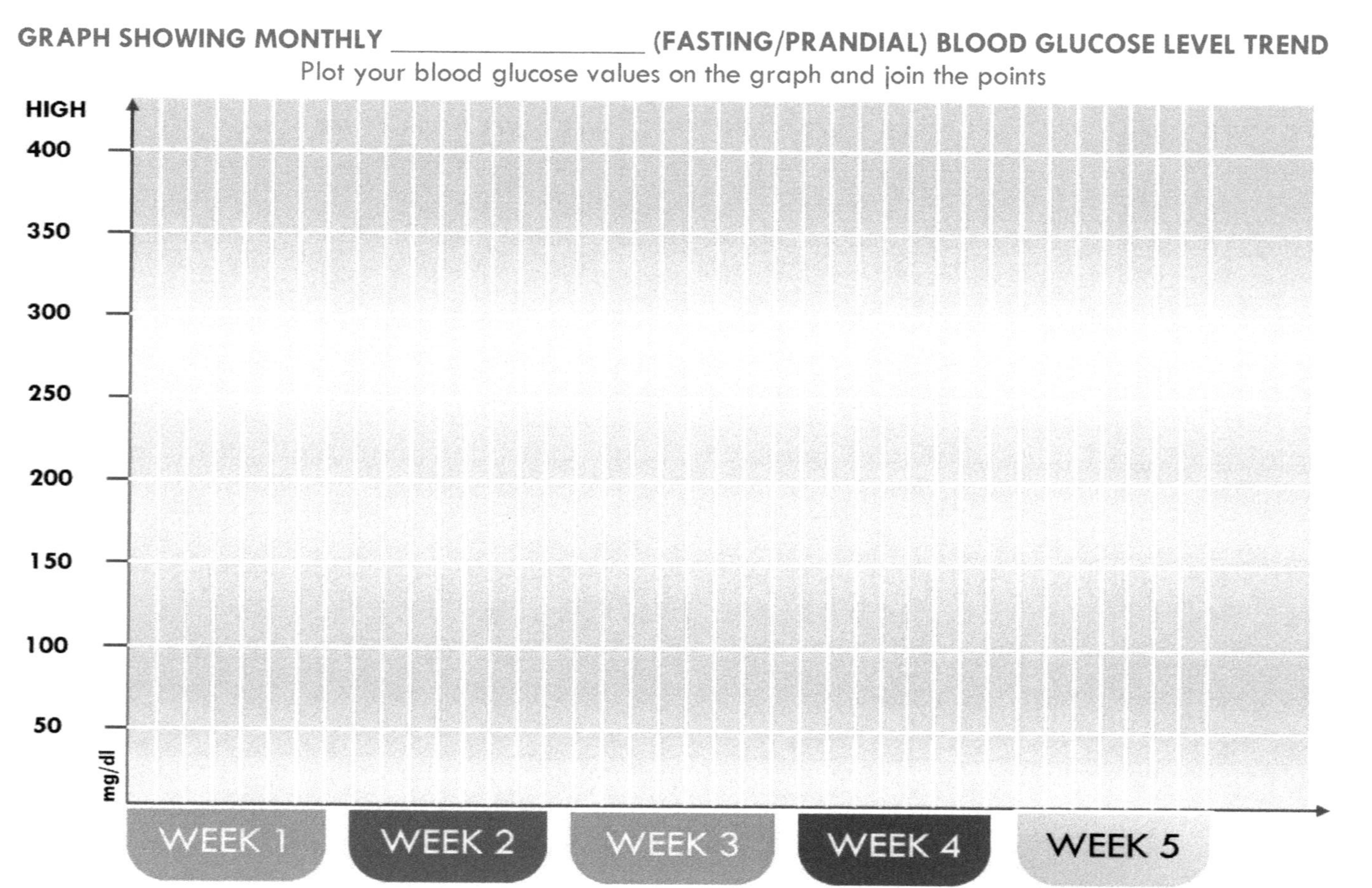

MONTHLY SUMMARY

GRAPH SHOWING MONTHLY _________________ (FASTING/PRANDIAL) BLOOD GLUCOSE LEVEL TREND

Plot your blood glucose values on the graph and join the points

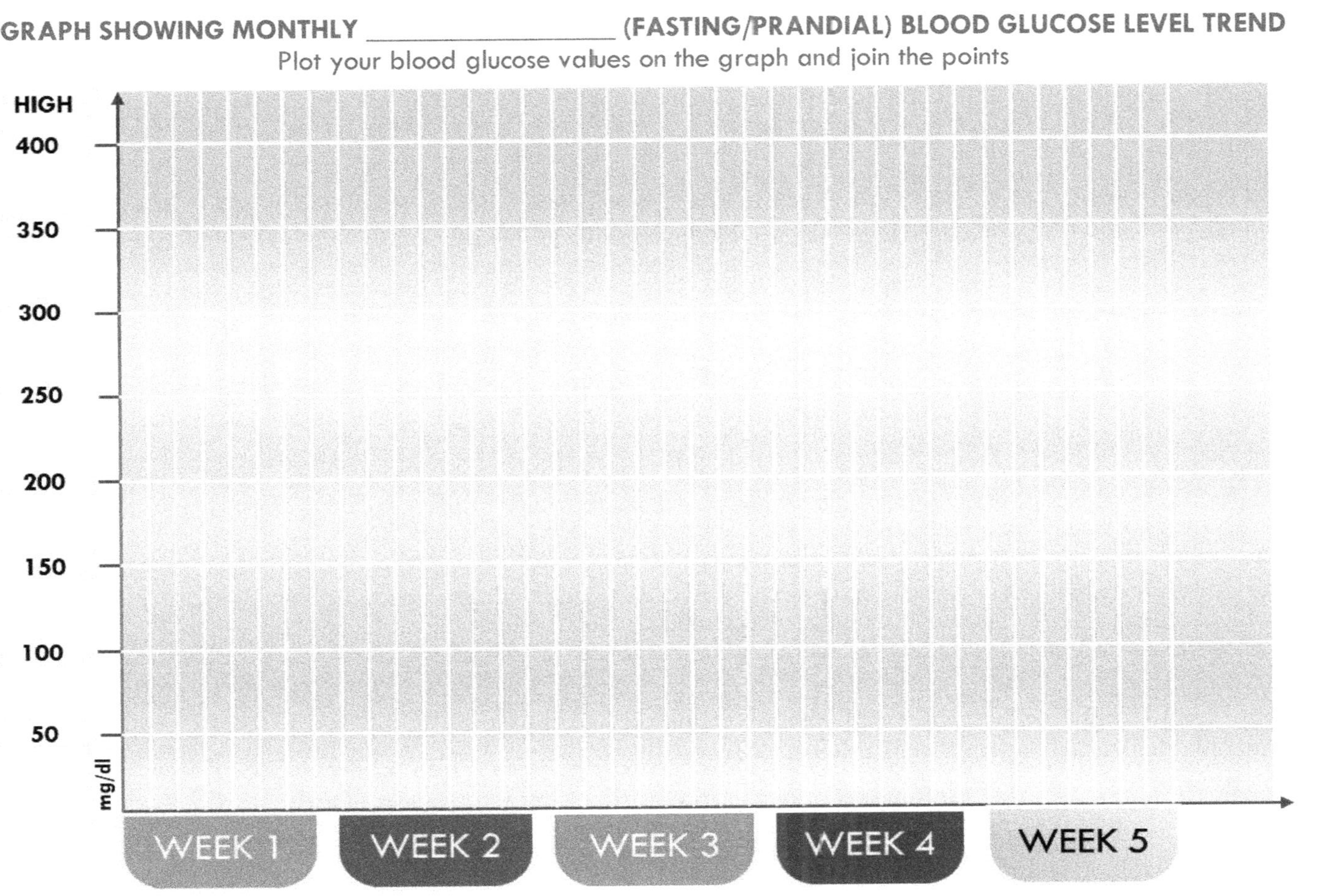

MONTHLY SUMMARY

Reflections on diet, exercise, and overall health

Any changes in medication or lifestyle

Goals for the next month

Points to discuss with my doctor

HYPERTENSION FACTS

Blood Pressure Categories

BLOOD PRESSURE CATEGORY	SYSTOLIC mm Hg (upper number)		DIASTOLIC mm Hg (lower number)
NORMAL	LESS THAN 120	and	LESS THAN 80
ELEVATED	120 – 129	and	LESS THAN 80
HIGH BLOOD PRESSURE (HYPERTENSION) STAGE 1	130 – 139	or	80 – 89
HIGH BLOOD PRESSURE (HYPERTENSION) STAGE 2	140 OR HIGHER	or	90 OR HIGHER
HYPERTENSIVE CRISIS (consult your doctor immediately)	HIGHER THAN 180	and/or	HIGHER THAN 120

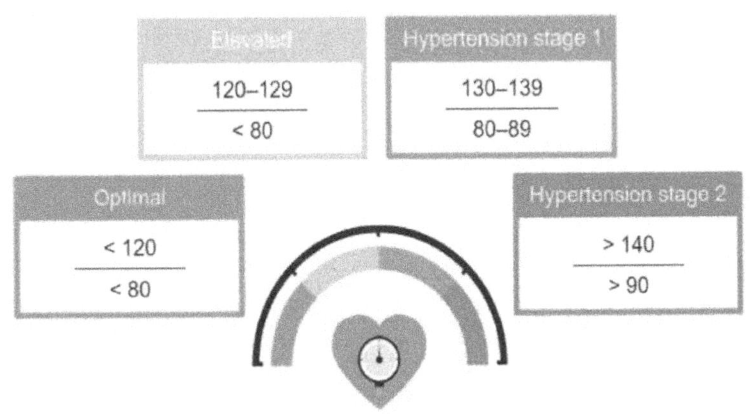

Date			Day
Time	Blood sugar (mg/dl)	Blood pressure (mmHg)	Insulin dose/Notes
Morning (Fasting)			
Before Lunch			
After Lunch			
Evening (Before dinner)			
Before Bed (after dinner)			
Midnight			

Date			Day
Morning (Fasting)			
Before Lunch			
After Lunch			
Evening (Before dinner)			
Before Bed (after dinner)			
Midnight			

Date			Day
Morning (Fasting)			
Before Lunch			
After Lunch			
Evening (Before dinner)			
Before Bed (after dinner)			
Midnight			

Other information

Date			Day
Time	Blood sugar (mg/dl)	Blood pressure (mmHg)	Insulin dose/Notes
Morning (Fasting)			
Before Lunch			
After Lunch			
Evening (Before dinner)			
Before Bed (after dinner)			
Midnight			

Date			Day
Morning (Fasting)			
Before Lunch			
After Lunch			
Evening (Before dinner)			
Before Bed (after dinner)			
Midnight			

Date			Day
Morning (Fasting)			
Before Lunch			
After Lunch			
Evening (Before dinner)			
Before Bed (after dinner)			
Midnight			

Other information

Date			Day
Time	Blood sugar (mg/dl)	Blood pressure (mmHg)	Insulin dose/Notes
Morning (Fasting)			
Before Lunch			
After Lunch			
Evening (Before dinner)			
Before Bed (after dinner)			
Midnight			

Date			Day
Morning (Fasting)			
Before Lunch			
After Lunch			
Evening (Before dinner)			
Before Bed (after dinner)			
Midnight			

Date			Day
Morning (Fasting)			
Before Lunch			
After Lunch			
Evening (Before dinner)			
Before Bed (after dinner)			
Midnight			

Other information

WEEKLY SUMMARY

Weekly readings Summary

Day	Fasting	Before lunch	After lunch	Evening before dinner	After dinner	Midnight	Blood pressure
Average							

Reflections on diet, exercise, and overall health

Any changes in medication or lifestyle

Goals for the next week

Date		**Day**	
Time	Blood sugar (mg/dl)	Blood pressure (mmHg)	Insulin dose/Notes
Morning (Fasting)			
Before Lunch			
After Lunch			
Evening (Before dinner)			
Before Bed (after dinner)			
Midnight			

Date		**Day**	
Morning (Fasting)			
Before Lunch			
After Lunch			
Evening (Before dinner)			
Before Bed (after dinner)			
Midnight			

Date		**Day**	
Morning (Fasting)			
Before Lunch			
After Lunch			
Evening (Before dinner)			
Before Bed (after dinner)			
Midnight			

Other information

Date		Day	
Time	Blood sugar (mg/dl)	Blood pressure (mmHg)	Insulin dose/Notes
Morning (Fasting)			
Before Lunch			
After Lunch			
Evening (Before dinner)			
Before Bed (after dinner)			
Midnight			

Date		Day	
Morning (Fasting)			
Before Lunch			
After Lunch			
Evening (Before dinner)			
Before Bed (after dinner)			
Midnight			

Date		Day	
Morning (Fasting)			
Before Lunch			
After Lunch			
Evening (Before dinner)			
Before Bed (after dinner)			
Midnight			

Other information

Date		Day	
Time	Blood sugar (mg/dl)	Blood pressure (mmHg)	Insulin dose/Notes
Morning (Fasting)			
Before Lunch			
After Lunch			
Evening (Before dinner)			
Before Bed (after dinner)			
Midnight			

Date		Day	
Morning (Fasting)			
Before Lunch			
After Lunch			
Evening (Before dinner)			
Before Bed (after dinner)			
Midnight			

Date		Day	
Morning (Fasting)			
Before Lunch			
After Lunch			
Evening (Before dinner)			
Before Bed (after dinner)			
Midnight			

Other information

WEEKLY SUMMARY

Weekly readings Summary							
Day	Fasting	Before lunch	After lunch	Evening before dinner	After dinner	Midnight	Blood pressure
Average							

Reflections on diet, exercise, and overall health

Any changes in medication or lifestyle

Goals for the next week

Date			**Day**
Time	Blood sugar (mg/dl)	Blood pressure (mmHg)	Insulin dose/Notes
Morning (Fasting)			
Before Lunch			
After Lunch			
Evening (Before dinner)			
Before Bed (after dinner)			
Midnight			

Date			**Day**
Morning (Fasting)			
Before Lunch			
After Lunch			
Evening (Before dinner)			
Before Bed (after dinner)			
Midnight			

Date			**Day**
Morning (Fasting)			
Before Lunch			
After Lunch			
Evening (Before dinner)			
Before Bed (after dinner)			
Midnight			

Other information

Date			Day
Time	Blood sugar (mg/dl)	Blood pressure (mmHg)	Insulin dose/Notes
Morning (Fasting)			
Before Lunch			
After Lunch			
Evening (Before dinner)			
Before Bed (after dinner)			
Midnight			

Date			Day
Morning (Fasting)			
Before Lunch			
After Lunch			
Evening (Before dinner)			
Before Bed (after dinner)			
Midnight			

Date			Day
Morning (Fasting)			
Before Lunch			
After Lunch			
Evening (Before dinner)			
Before Bed (after dinner)			
Midnight			

Other information

Date		Day	
Time	Blood sugar (mg/dl)	Blood pressure (mmHg)	Insulin dose/Notes
Morning (Fasting)			
Before Lunch			
After Lunch			
Evening (Before dinner)			
Before Bed (after dinner)			
Midnight			

Date		Day	
Morning (Fasting)			
Before Lunch			
After Lunch			
Evening (Before dinner)			
Before Bed (after dinner)			
Midnight			

Date		Day	
Morning (Fasting)			
Before Lunch			
After Lunch			
Evening (Before dinner)			
Before Bed (after dinner)			
Midnight			

Other information

WEEKLY SUMMARY

Weekly readings Summary

Day	Fasting	Before lunch	After lunch	Evening before dinner	After dinner	Midnight	Blood pressure
Average							

Reflections on diet, exercise, and overall health

Any changes in medication or lifestyle

Goals for the next week

Date		Day	
Time	Blood sugar (mg/dl)	Blood pressure (mmHg)	Insulin dose/Notes
Morning (Fasting)			
Before Lunch			
After Lunch			
Evening (Before dinner)			
Before Bed (after dinner)			
Midnight			

Date		Day	
Morning (Fasting)			
Before Lunch			
After Lunch			
Evening (Before dinner)			
Before Bed (after dinner)			
Midnight			

Date		Day	
Morning (Fasting)			
Before Lunch			
After Lunch			
Evening (Before dinner)			
Before Bed (after dinner)			
Midnight			

Other information

Date			Day
Time	Blood sugar (mg/dl)	Blood pressure (mmHg)	Insulin dose/Notes
Morning (Fasting)			
Before Lunch			
After Lunch			
Evening (Before dinner)			
Before Bed (after dinner)			
Midnight			

Date			Day
Morning (Fasting)			
Before Lunch			
After Lunch			
Evening (Before dinner)			
Before Bed (after dinner)			
Midnight			

Date			Day
Morning (Fasting)			
Before Lunch			
After Lunch			
Evening (Before dinner)			
Before Bed (after dinner)			
Midnight			

Other information

Date			Day
Time	Blood sugar (mg/dl)	Blood pressure (mmHg)	Insulin dose/Notes
Morning (Fasting)			
Before Lunch			
After Lunch			
Evening (Before dinner)			
Before Bed (after dinner)			
Midnight			

Date			Day
Morning (Fasting)			
Before Lunch			
After Lunch			
Evening (Before dinner)			
Before Bed (after dinner)			
Midnight			

Date			Day
Morning (Fasting)			
Before Lunch			
After Lunch			
Evening (Before dinner)			
Before Bed (after dinner)			
Midnight			

Other information

WEEKLY SUMMARY

Weekly readings Summary

Day	Fasting	Before lunch	After lunch	Evening before dinner	After dinner	Midnight	Blood pressure
Average							

Reflections on diet, exercise, and overall health

Any changes in medication or lifestyle

Goals for the next week

MONTHLY SUMMARY

GRAPH SHOWING MONTHLY _________________ (FASTING/PRANDIAL) BLOOD GLUCOSE LEVEL TREND

Plot your blood glucose values on the graph and join the points

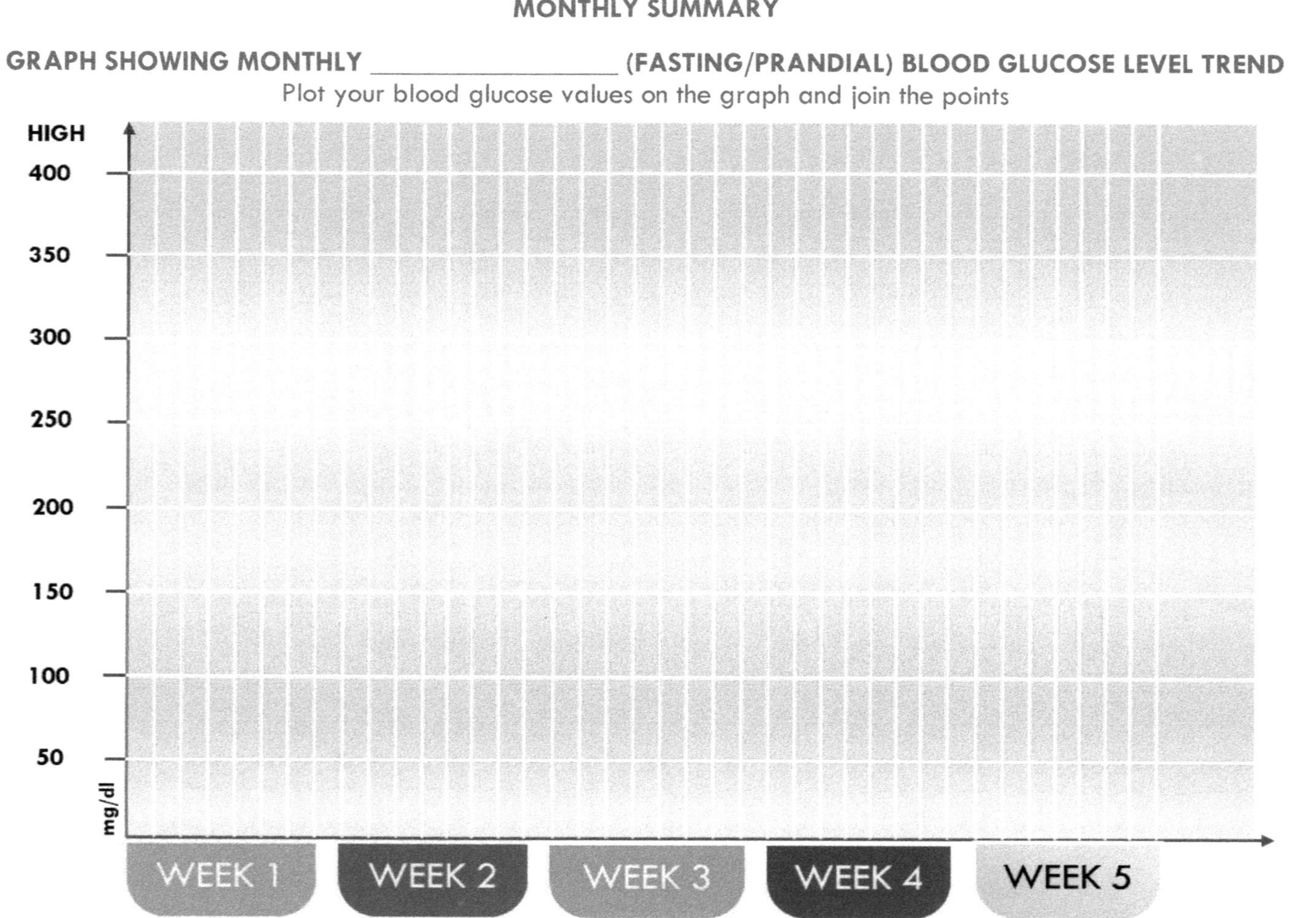

MONTHLY SUMMARY

GRAPH SHOWING MONTHLY _________________ (FASTING/PRANDIAL) BLOOD GLUCOSE LEVEL TREND

Plot your blood glucose values on the graph and join the points

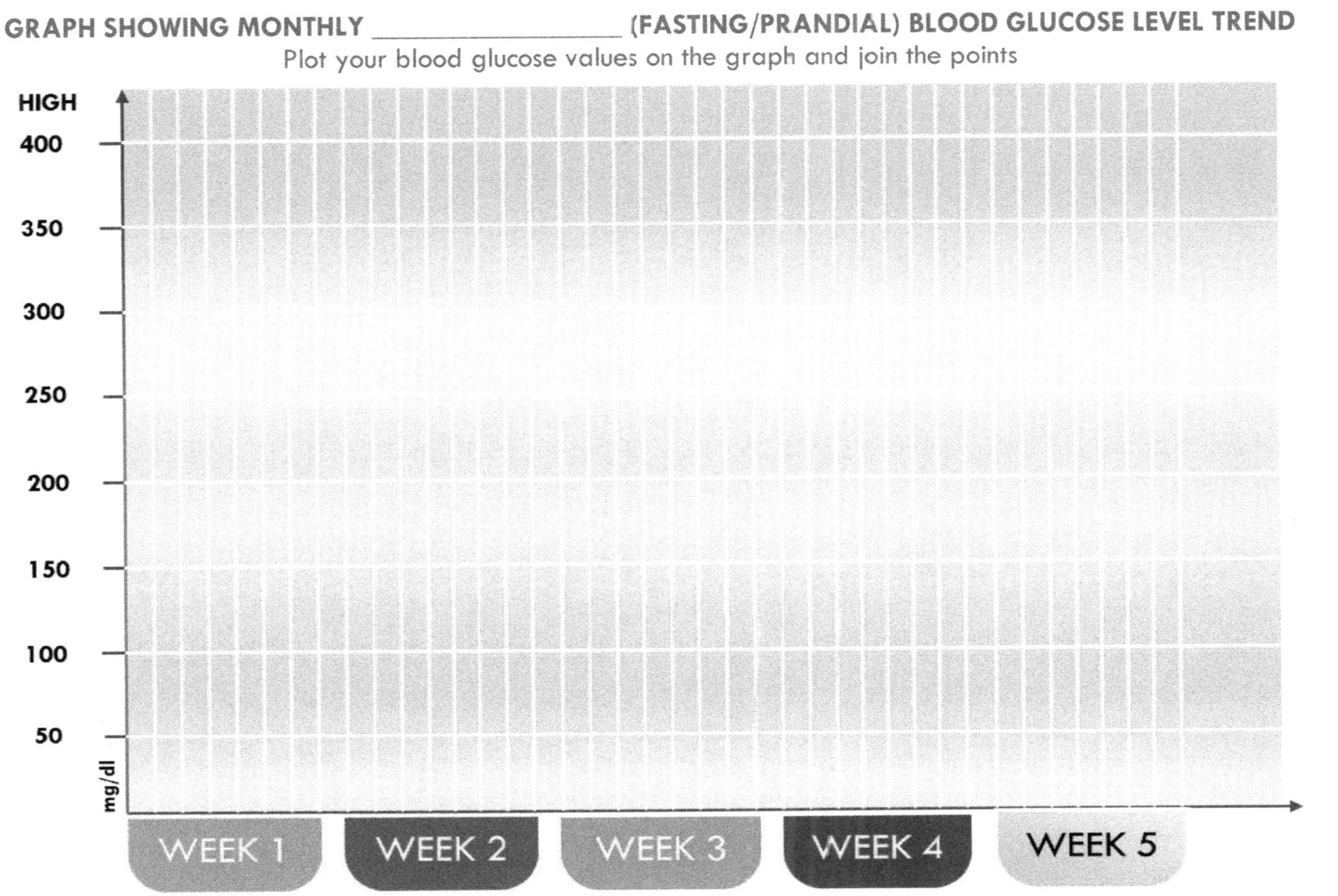

MONTHLY SUMMARY

Reflections on diet, exercise, and overall health

Any changes in medication or lifestyle

Goals for the next month

Points to discuss with my doctor

HOW TO MEASURE BLOOD PRESSURE USING AN ELECTRONIC BP APPARATUS

Follow these steps to accurately measure blood pressure using an electronic blood pressure monitor:

1. Prepare the Equipment and Yourself

2. Ensure you have a properly functioning electronic blood pressure monitor with a cuff that fits your arm.
- Sit quietly and rest for 5 minutes before taking the measurement.
- Avoid caffeine, exercise, and smoking 30 minutes before measurement.
- Sit in the Right Position

3. Sit in a chair with your back supported and feet flat on the floor. Place your arm on a table so that the cuff is at heart level. Make sure your arm is relaxed and not tense. Apply the Cuff

4. Wrap the cuff snugly around your upper arm. The bottom edge of the cuff should be about 1 inch (2-3 cm) above the bend of your elbow. Ensure the cuff is not too tight or too loose; you should be able to slip two fingers under the cuff.

5. Position the Monitor -Place the monitor on a stable, flat surface near your arm. Ensure that the tube connecting the cuff to the monitor is not twisted or pinched.

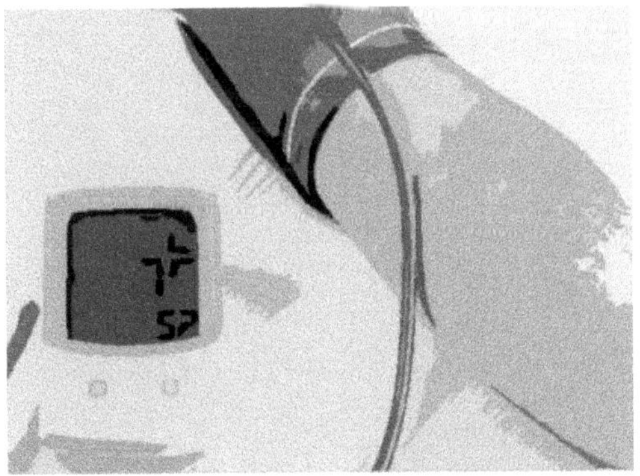

6. Start the Measurement - Press the power button to turn on the monitor. Press the start button to begin the measurement. The cuff will inflate automatically. Remain still and do not talk while the measurement is being taken. Read the Results.

7. The monitor will display your systolic and diastolic blood pressure readings along with your pulse rate. Note down the readings, including the date and time. Take Multiple Readings.

8. For accuracy, take 2-3 readings at one-minute intervals and record the average.

9. Record Your Readings. Maintain a blood pressure logbook to track your readings over time. Include the date, time, and any relevant notes (e.g., feeling stressed or unwell).

10. Turn Off the Monitor. Turn off the monitor to save battery life. Some monitors may turn off automatically after a few minutes. Store the Equipment Store your blood pressure monitor and cuff in a cool, dry place.

Date		Day	
Time	Blood sugar (mg/dl)	Blood pressure (mmHg)	Insulin dose/Notes
Morning (Fasting)			
Before Lunch			
After Lunch			
Evening (Before dinner)			
Before Bed (after dinner)			
Midnight			

Date		Day	
Morning (Fasting)			
Before Lunch			
After Lunch			
Evening (Before dinner)			
Before Bed (after dinner)			
Midnight			

Date		Day	
Morning (Fasting)			
Before Lunch			
After Lunch			
Evening (Before dinner)			
Before Bed (after dinner)			
Midnight			

Other information

Date			Day
Time	Blood sugar (mg/dl)	Blood pressure (mmHg)	Insulin dose/Notes
Morning (Fasting)			
Before Lunch			
After Lunch			
Evening (Before dinner)			
Before Bed (after dinner)			
Midnight			

Date			Day
Morning (Fasting)			
Before Lunch			
After Lunch			
Evening (Before dinner)			
Before Bed (after dinner)			
Midnight			

Date			Day
Morning (Fasting)			
Before Lunch			
After Lunch			
Evening (Before dinner)			
Before Bed (after dinner)			
Midnight			

Other information

Date		Day	
Time	Blood sugar (mg/dl)	Blood pressure (mmHg)	Insulin dose/Notes
Morning (Fasting)			
Before Lunch			
After Lunch			
Evening (Before dinner)			
Before Bed (after dinner)			
Midnight			

Date		Day	
Morning (Fasting)			
Before Lunch			
After Lunch			
Evening (Before dinner)			
Before Bed (after dinner)			
Midnight			

Date		Day	
Morning (Fasting)			
Before Lunch			
After Lunch			
Evening (Before dinner)			
Before Bed (after dinner)			
Midnight			

Other information

WEEKLY SUMMARY

	Weekly readings Summary						
Day	Fasting	Before lunch	After lunch	Evening before dinner	After dinner	Midnight	Blood pressure
Average							

Reflections on diet, exercise, and overall health

Any changes in medication or lifestyle

Goals for the next week

Date			Day
Time	Blood sugar (mg/dl)	Blood pressure (mmHg)	Insulin dose/Notes
Morning (Fasting)			
Before Lunch			
After Lunch			
Evening (Before dinner)			
Before Bed (after dinner)			
Midnight			
Date			Day
Morning (Fasting)			
Before Lunch			
After Lunch			
Evening (Before dinner)			
Before Bed (after dinner)			
Midnight			
Date			Day
Morning (Fasting)			
Before Lunch			
After Lunch			
Evening (Before dinner)			
Before Bed (after dinner)			
Midnight			

Other information

Date			Day
Time	Blood sugar (mg/dl)	Blood pressure (mmHg)	Insulin dose/Notes
Morning (Fasting)			
Before Lunch			
After Lunch			
Evening (Before dinner)			
Before Bed (after dinner)			
Midnight			

Date			Day
Morning (Fasting)			
Before Lunch			
After Lunch			
Evening (Before dinner)			
Before Bed (after dinner)			
Midnight			

Date			Day
Morning (Fasting)			
Before Lunch			
After Lunch			
Evening (Before dinner)			
Before Bed (after dinner)			
Midnight			

Other information

Date		Day	
Time	Blood sugar (mg/dl)	Blood pressure (mmHg)	Insulin dose/Notes
Morning (Fasting)			
Before Lunch			
After Lunch			
Evening (Before dinner)			
Before Bed (after dinner)			
Midnight			

Date		Day	
Morning (Fasting)			
Before Lunch			
After Lunch			
Evening (Before dinner)			
Before Bed (after dinner)			
Midnight			

Date		Day	
Morning (Fasting)			
Before Lunch			
After Lunch			
Evening (Before dinner)			
Before Bed (after dinner)			
Midnight			

Other information

WEEKLY SUMMARY

Weekly readings Summary

Day	Fasting	Before lunch	After lunch	Evening before dinner	After dinner	Midnight	Blood pressure
Average							

Reflections on diet, exercise, and overall health

Any changes in medication or lifestyle

Goals for the next week

Date			Day
Time	Blood sugar (mg/dl)	Blood pressure (mmHg)	Insulin dose/Notes
Morning (Fasting)			
Before Lunch			
After Lunch			
Evening (Before dinner)			
Before Bed (after dinner)			
Midnight			

Date			Day
Morning (Fasting)			
Before Lunch			
After Lunch			
Evening (Before dinner)			
Before Bed (after dinner)			
Midnight			

Date			Day
Morning (Fasting)			
Before Lunch			
After Lunch			
Evening (Before dinner)			
Before Bed (after dinner)			
Midnight			

Other information

Date		Day	
Time	Blood sugar (mg/dl)	Blood pressure (mmHg)	Insulin dose/Notes
Morning (Fasting)			
Before Lunch			
After Lunch			
Evening (Before dinner)			
Before Bed (after dinner)			
Midnight			

Date		Day	
Morning (Fasting)			
Before Lunch			
After Lunch			
Evening (Before dinner)			
Before Bed (after dinner)			
Midnight			

Date		Day	
Morning (Fasting)			
Before Lunch			
After Lunch			
Evening (Before dinner)			
Before Bed (after dinner)			
Midnight			

Other information

Date		Day	
Time	Blood sugar (mg/dl)	Blood pressure (mmHg)	Insulin dose/Notes
Morning (Fasting)			
Before Lunch			
After Lunch			
Evening (Before dinner)			
Before Bed (after dinner)			
Midnight			

Date		Day	
Morning (Fasting)			
Before Lunch			
After Lunch			
Evening (Before dinner)			
Before Bed (after dinner)			
Midnight			

Date		Day	
Morning (Fasting)			
Before Lunch			
After Lunch			
Evening (Before dinner)			
Before Bed (after dinner)			
Midnight			

Other information

WEEKLY SUMMARY

Weekly readings Summary

Day	Fasting	Before lunch	After lunch	Evening before dinner	After dinner	Midnight	Blood pressure
Average							

Reflections on diet, exercise, and overall health

Any changes in medication or lifestyle

Goals for the next week

Date			Day
Time	Blood sugar (mg/dl)	Blood pressure (mmHg)	Insulin dose/Notes
Morning (Fasting)			
Before Lunch			
After Lunch			
Evening (Before dinner)			
Before Bed (after dinner)			
Midnight			

Date			Day
Morning (Fasting)			
Before Lunch			
After Lunch			
Evening (Before dinner)			
Before Bed (after dinner)			
Midnight			

Date			Day
Morning (Fasting)			
Before Lunch			
After Lunch			
Evening (Before dinner)			
Before Bed (after dinner)			
Midnight			

Other information

Date			Day
Time	Blood sugar (mg/dl)	Blood pressure (mmHg)	Insulin dose/Notes
Morning (Fasting)			
Before Lunch			
After Lunch			
Evening (Before dinner)			
Before Bed (after dinner)			
Midnight			
Date			**Day**
Morning (Fasting)			
Before Lunch			
After Lunch			
Evening (Before dinner)			
Before Bed (after dinner)			
Midnight			
Date			**Day**
Morning (Fasting)			
Before Lunch			
After Lunch			
Evening (Before dinner)			
Before Bed (after dinner)			
Midnight			
Other information			

Date		**Day**	
Time	Blood sugar (mg/dl)	Blood pressure (mmHg)	Insulin dose/Notes
Morning (Fasting)			
Before Lunch			
After Lunch			
Evening (Before dinner)			
Before Bed (after dinner)			
Midnight			

Date		**Day**	
Morning (Fasting)			
Before Lunch			
After Lunch			
Evening (Before dinner)			
Before Bed (after dinner)			
Midnight			

Date		**Day**	
Morning (Fasting)			
Before Lunch			
After Lunch			
Evening (Before dinner)			
Before Bed (after dinner)			
Midnight			

Other information

Weekly readings Summary

Day	Fasting	Before lunch	After lunch	Evening before dinner	After dinner	Midnight	Blood pressure
Average							

Reflections on diet, exercise, and overall health

Any changes in medication or lifestyle

Goals for the next week

MONTHLY SUMMARY

GRAPH SHOWING MONTHLY _________________ (FASTING/PRANDIAL) BLOOD GLUCOSE LEVEL TREND

Plot your blood glucose values on the graph and join the points

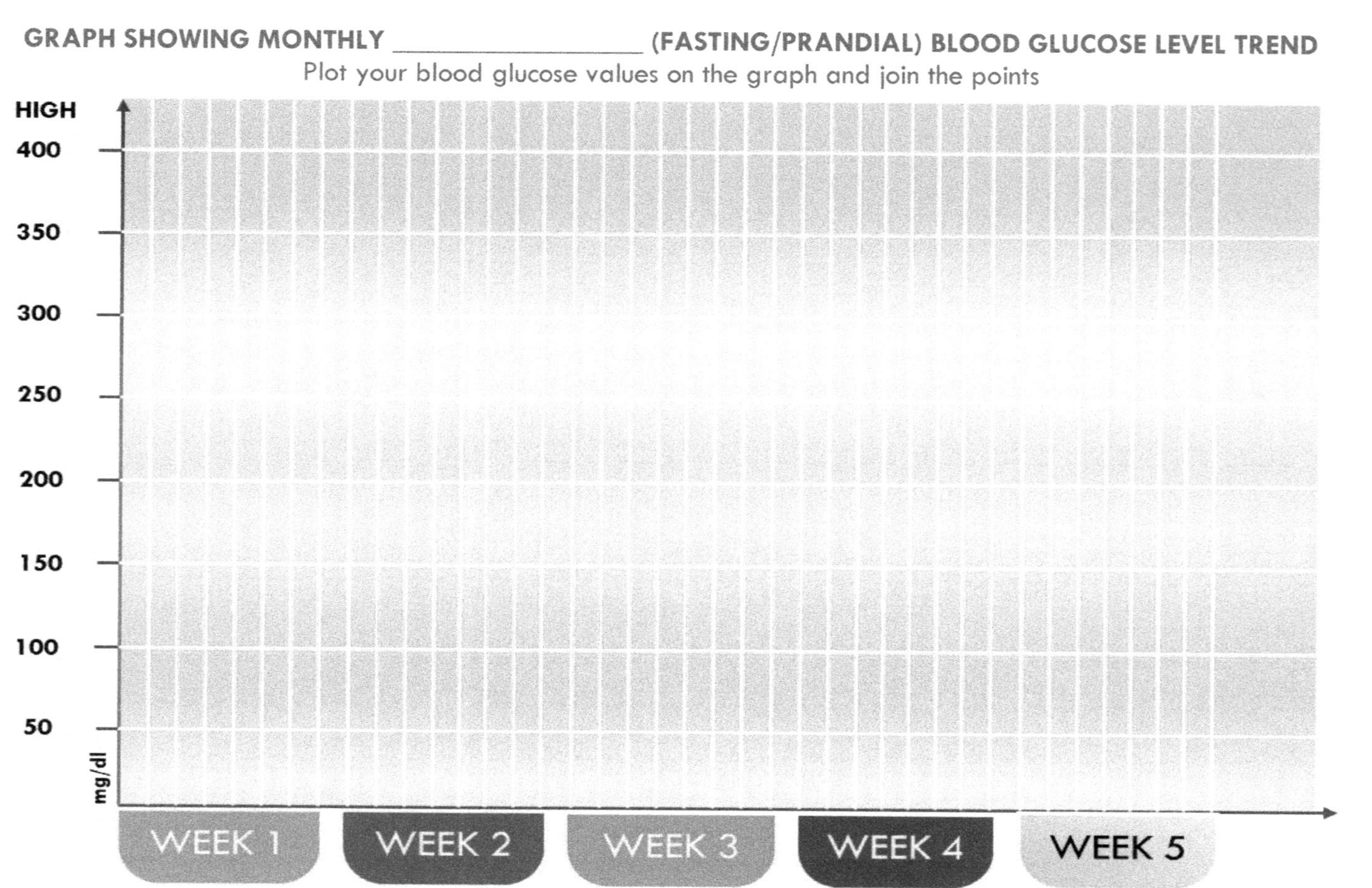

MONTHLY SUMMARY

GRAPH SHOWING MONTHLY _________________ (FASTING/PRANDIAL) BLOOD GLUCOSE LEVEL TREND

Plot your blood glucose values on the graph and join the points

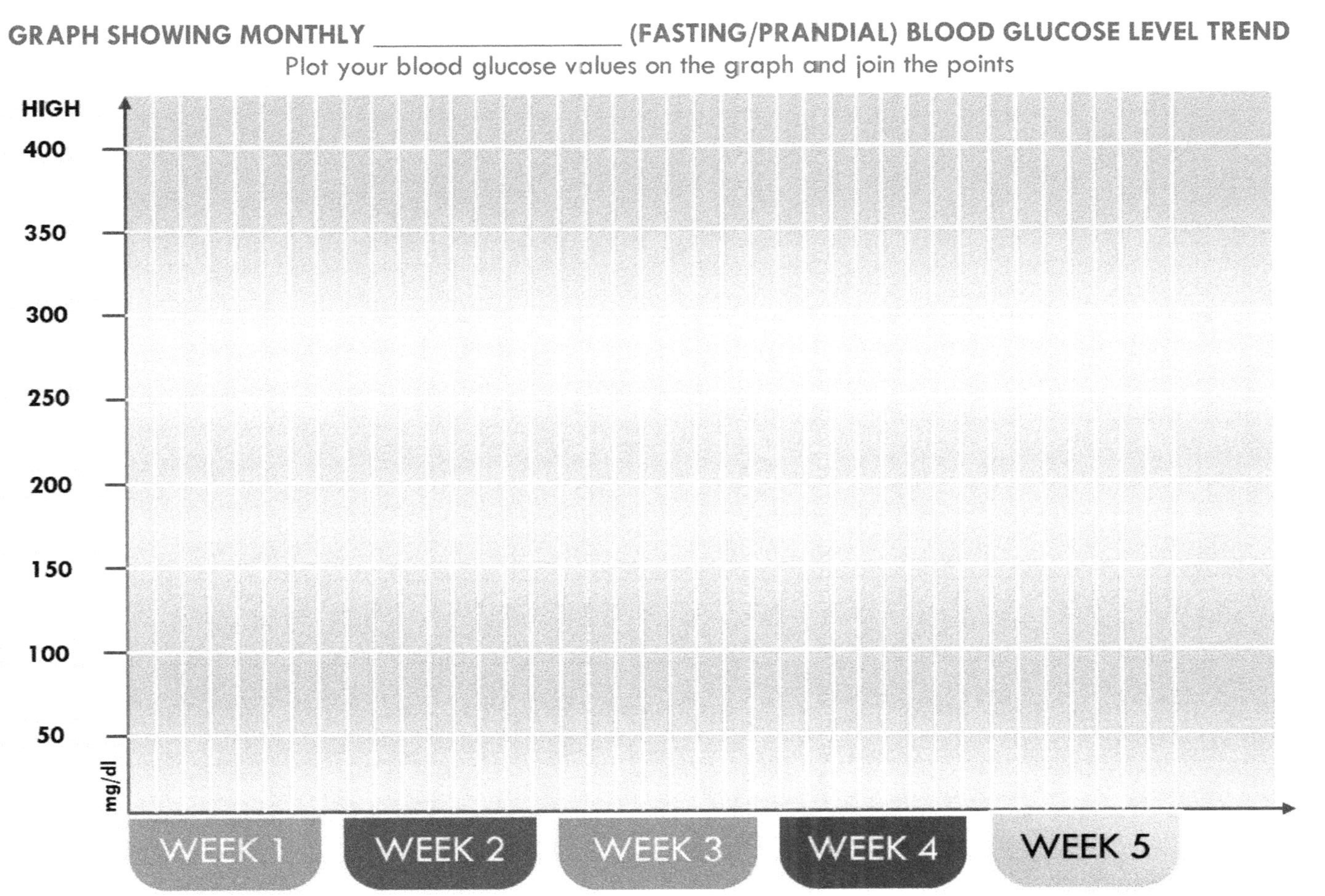

MONTHLY SUMMARY

Reflections on diet, exercise, and overall health

Any changes in medication or lifestyle

Goals for the next month

Points to discuss with my doctor

Here are the steps for checking blood glucose using a glucometer

1. Wash and Dry Hands : Wash your hands with soap and warm water, and then dry them thoroughly. This helps prevent infection and ensures accurate readings.

2. Prepare the Glucometer and Supplies
- Gather your glucometer, a test strip, a lancet, and a lancing device.
- Turn on the glucometer if it requires manual activation.
- Insert a test strip into the glucometer as per the device's instructions.

3. Prepare the Lancing Device
- Insert a new lancet into the lancing device and adjust the depth setting if necessary.
- Prime the lancing device by pulling back the lever until it clicks.

4. Prick Your Finger:
- Select a site on the side of your fingertip (avoiding the pad).
- Press the lancing device against the chosen site and press the release button to prick your finger.

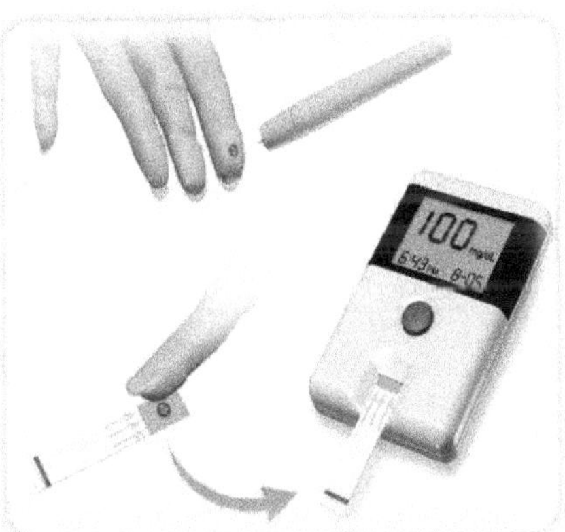

5. Obtain a Blood Sample:
- Gently squeeze or massage your finger from the base to the tip to obtain a drop of blood.
- Ensure the blood drop is sufficient for the test strip to absorb.

6. Apply the Blood Sample to the Test Strip:
- Touch the edge of the test strip to the blood drop. The strip will draw in the blood through capillary action.
- Wait for the glucometer to process the sample. This usually takes a few seconds.

7. Read and Record the Result:
- Once the glucometer displays the reading, note the blood glucose level.
- Record the result in a logbook including the time and any relevant notes (e.g., fasting, before/after meals).

8. Dispose of Used Supplies Safely:
- Dispose of the used lancet and test strip in a proper sharps container.
- Clean the lancing device and glucometer if needed.

9. Store Your Supplies :
- Store your glucometer, lancets, and test strips in a cool, dry place.

By following these steps, you can accurately monitor your blood glucose levels at home.

Date			**Day**
Time	Blood sugar (mg/dl)	Blood pressure (mmHg)	Insulin dose/Notes
Morning (Fasting)			
Before Lunch			
After Lunch			
Evening (Before dinner)			
Before Bed (after dinner)			
Midnight			

Date			**Day**
Morning (Fasting)			
Before Lunch			
After Lunch			
Evening (Before dinner)			
Before Bed (after dinner)			
Midnight			

Date			**Day**
Morning (Fasting)			
Before Lunch			
After Lunch			
Evening (Before dinner)			
Before Bed (after dinner)			
Midnight			

Other information

Date			Day
Time	Blood sugar (mg/dl)	Blood pressure (mmHg)	Insulin dose/Notes
Morning (Fasting)			
Before Lunch			
After Lunch			
Evening (Before dinner)			
Before Bed (after dinner)			
Midnight			

Date			Day
Morning (Fasting)			
Before Lunch			
After Lunch			
Evening (Before dinner)			
Before Bed (after dinner)			
Midnight			

Date			Day
Morning (Fasting)			
Before Lunch			
After Lunch			
Evening (Before dinner)			
Before Bed (after dinner)			
Midnight			

Other information

Date		Day	
Time	Blood sugar (mg/dl)	Blood pressure (mmHg)	Insulin dose/Notes
Morning (Fasting)			
Before Lunch			
After Lunch			
Evening (Before dinner)			
Before Bed (after dinner)			
Midnight			

Date		Day	
Morning (Fasting)			
Before Lunch			
After Lunch			
Evening (Before dinner)			
Before Bed (after dinner)			
Midnight			

Date		Day	
Morning (Fasting)			
Before Lunch			
After Lunch			
Evening (Before dinner)			
Before Bed (after dinner)			
Midnight			

Other information

WEEKLY SUMMARY

Weekly readings Summary

Day	Fasting	Before lunch	After lunch	Evening before dinner	After dinner	Midnight	Blood pressure
Average							

Reflections on diet, exercise, and overall health

Any changes in medication or lifestyle

Goals for the next week

Date			Day
Time	Blood sugar (mg/dl)	Blood pressure (mmHg)	Insulin dose/Notes
Morning (Fasting)			
Before Lunch			
After Lunch			
Evening (Before dinner)			
Before Bed (after dinner)			
Midnight			

Date			Day
Morning (Fasting)			
Before Lunch			
After Lunch			
Evening (Before dinner)			
Before Bed (after dinner)			
Midnight			

Date			Day
Morning (Fasting)			
Before Lunch			
After Lunch			
Evening (Before dinner)			
Before Bed (after dinner)			
Midnight			

Other information

Date			Day
Time	Blood sugar (mg/dl)	Blood pressure (mmHg)	Insulin dose/Notes
Morning (Fasting)			
Before Lunch			
After Lunch			
Evening (Before dinner)			
Before Bed (after dinner)			
Midnight			

Date			Day
Morning (Fasting)			
Before Lunch			
After Lunch			
Evening (Before dinner)			
Before Bed (after dinner)			
Midnight			

Date			Day
Morning (Fasting)			
Before Lunch			
After Lunch			
Evening (Before dinner)			
Before Bed (after dinner)			
Midnight			

Other information

Date		Day	
Time	Blood sugar (mg/dl)	Blood pressure (mmHg)	Insulin dose/Notes
Morning (Fasting)			
Before Lunch			
After Lunch			
Evening (Before dinner)			
Before Bed (after dinner)			
Midnight			

Date		Day	
Morning (Fasting)			
Before Lunch			
After Lunch			
Evening (Before dinner)			
Before Bed (after dinner)			
Midnight			

Date		Day	
Morning (Fasting)			
Before Lunch			
After Lunch			
Evening (Before dinner)			
Before Bed (after dinner)			
Midnight			

Other information

WEEKLY SUMMARY

Day	Fasting	Before lunch	After lunch	Evening before dinner	After dinner	Midnight	Blood pressure
Average							

Reflections on diet, exercise, and overall health

Any changes in medication or lifestyle

Goals for the next week

Date			Day
Time	Blood sugar (mg/dl)	Blood pressure (mmHg)	Insulin dose/Notes
Morning (Fasting)			
Before Lunch			
After Lunch			
Evening (Before dinner)			
Before Bed (after dinner)			
Midnight			

Date			Day
Morning (Fasting)			
Before Lunch			
After Lunch			
Evening (Before dinner)			
Before Bed (after dinner)			
Midnight			

Date			Day
Morning (Fasting)			
Before Lunch			
After Lunch			
Evening (Before dinner)			
Before Bed (after dinner)			
Midnight			

Other information

Date			Day
Time	Blood sugar (mg/dl)	Blood pressure (mmHg)	Insulin dose/Notes
Morning (Fasting)			
Before Lunch			
After Lunch			
Evening (Before dinner)			
Before Bed (after dinner)			
Midnight			

Date			Day
Morning (Fasting)			
Before Lunch			
After Lunch			
Evening (Before dinner)			
Before Bed (after dinner)			
Midnight			

Date			Day
Morning (Fasting)			
Before Lunch			
After Lunch			
Evening (Before dinner)			
Before Bed (after dinner)			
Midnight			

Other information

Date		**Day**	
Time	Blood sugar (mg/dl)	Blood pressure (mmHg)	Insulin dose/Notes
Morning (Fasting)			
Before Lunch			
After Lunch			
Evening (Before dinner)			
Before Bed (after dinner)			
Midnight			

Date		**Day**	
Morning (Fasting)			
Before Lunch			
After Lunch			
Evening (Before dinner)			
Before Bed (after dinner)			
Midnight			

Date		**Day**	
Morning (Fasting)			
Before Lunch			
After Lunch			
Evening (Before dinner)			
Before Bed (after dinner)			
Midnight			

Other information

WEEKLY SUMMARY

Weekly readings Summary

Day	Fasting	Before lunch	After lunch	Evening before dinner	After dinner	Midnight	Blood pressure
Average							

Reflections on diet, exercise, and overall health

Any changes in medication or lifestyle

Goals for the next week

Date			Day
Time	Blood sugar (mg/dl)	Blood pressure (mmHg)	Insulin dose/Notes
Morning (Fasting)			
Before Lunch			
After Lunch			
Evening (Before dinner)			
Before Bed (after dinner)			
Midnight			

Date			Day
Morning (Fasting)			
Before Lunch			
After Lunch			
Evening (Before dinner)			
Before Bed (after dinner)			
Midnight			

Date			Day
Morning (Fasting)			
Before Lunch			
After Lunch			
Evening (Before dinner)			
Before Bed (after dinner)			
Midnight			

Other information

Date			Day
Time	Blood sugar (mg/dl)	Blood pressure (mmHg)	Insulin dose/Notes
Morning (Fasting)			
Before Lunch			
After Lunch			
Evening (Before dinner)			
Before Bed (after dinner)			
Midnight			

Date			Day
Morning (Fasting)			
Before Lunch			
After Lunch			
Evening (Before dinner)			
Before Bed (after dinner)			
Midnight			

Date			Day
Morning (Fasting)			
Before Lunch			
After Lunch			
Evening (Before dinner)			
Before Bed (after dinner)			
Midnight			

Other information

Date		**Day**	
Time	Blood sugar (mg/dl)	Blood pressure (mmHg)	Insulin dose/Notes
Morning (Fasting)			
Before Lunch			
After Lunch			
Evening (Before dinner)			
Before Bed (after dinner)			
Midnight			

Date		**Day**	
Morning (Fasting)			
Before Lunch			
After Lunch			
Evening (Before dinner)			
Before Bed (after dinner)			
Midnight			

Date		**Day**	
Morning (Fasting)			
Before Lunch			
After Lunch			
Evening (Before dinner)			
Before Bed (after dinner)			
Midnight			

Other information

WEEKLY SUMMARY

Day	Fasting	Before lunch	After lunch	Evening before dinner	After dinner	Midnight	Blood pressure
Average							

Weekly readings Summary

Reflections on diet, exercise, and overall health

Any changes in medication or lifestyle

Goals for the next week

MONTHLY SUMMARY

GRAPH SHOWING MONTHLY _________________ (FASTING/PRANDIAL) BLOOD GLUCOSE LEVEL TREND

Plot your blood glucose values on the graph and join the points

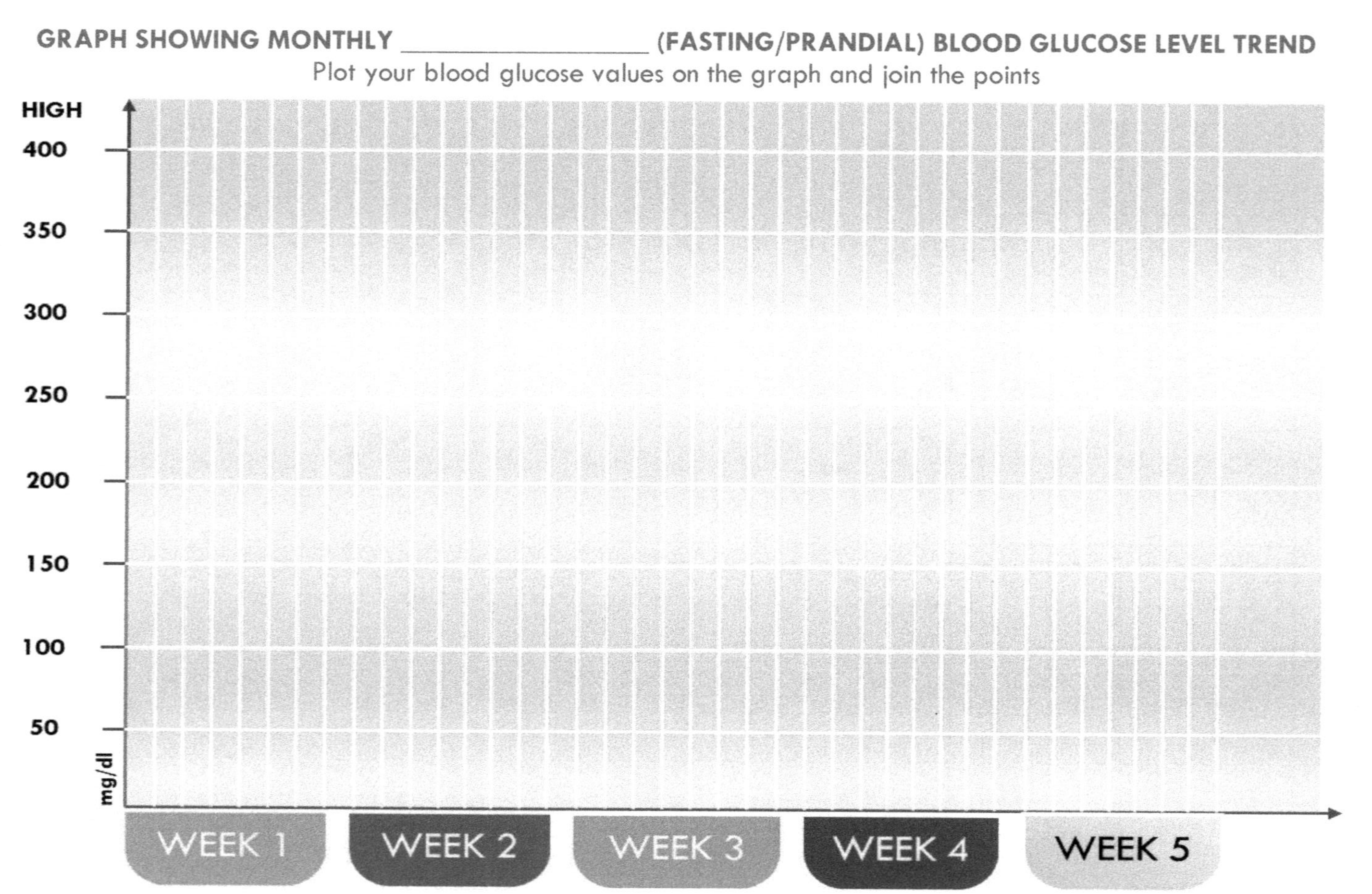

MONTHLY SUMMARY

GRAPH SHOWING MONTHLY _________________ (FASTING/PRANDIAL) BLOOD GLUCOSE LEVEL TREND

Plot your blood glucose values on the grcph and join the points

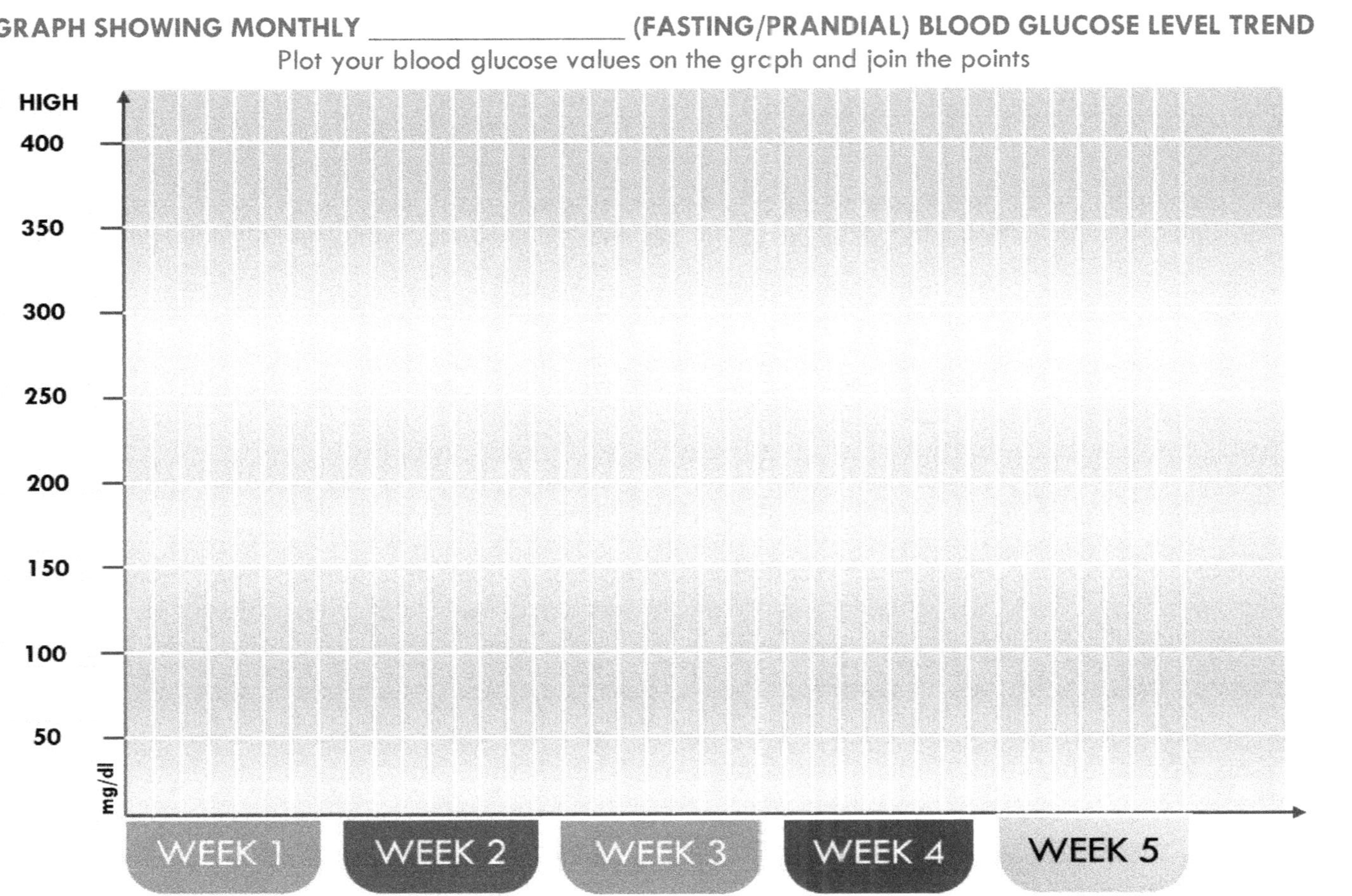

MONTHLY SUMMARY

Reflections on diet, exercise, and overall health

Any changes in medication or lifestyle

Goals for the next month

Points to discuss with my doctor

SICK DAY RULES FOR MANAGING DIABETES

1. Continue Medications
Do not stop taking insulin or oral medications unless advised by your healthcare provider

2. Monitor Blood Glucose Frequently
Check your blood glucose every 2-4 hours and keep a record.

3. Check for Ketones
Test your urine for ketones if blood glucose levels are above 240 mg/dL.

4. Stay Hydrated
Drink at least 8 ounces of sugar-free fluids every hour.

5. Adjust insulin dose
Adjust insulin doses as per your healthcare provider's recommendations.

6. Track symptoms
Monitor your symptoms and be alert for signs of diabetic ketoacidosis.

7. Rest & Self care
Get plenty of rest and take medications for symptoms as recommended.

Seek Medical Advice When Necessary

1. Blood glucose levels are consistently high or low.
2. Ketones are moderate to large.
3. Unable to keep fluids down.
4. Persistent diarrhea or vomiting.
5. Difficulty breathing or chest pain

Date			**Day**
Time	Blood sugar (mg/dl)	Blood pressure (mmHg)	Insulin dose/Notes
Morning (Fasting)			
Before Lunch			
After Lunch			
Evening (Before dinner)			
Before Bed (after dinner)			
Midnight			

Date			**Day**
Morning (Fasting)			
Before Lunch			
After Lunch			
Evening (Before dinner)			
Before Bed (after dinner)			
Midnight			

Date			**Day**
Morning (Fasting)			
Before Lunch			
After Lunch			
Evening (Before dinner)			
Before Bed (after dinner)			
Midnight			

Other information

Date			Day
Time	Blood sugar (mg/dl)	Blood pressure (mmHg)	Insulin dose/Notes
Morning (Fasting)			
Before Lunch			
After Lunch			
Evening (Before dinner)			
Before Bed (after dinner)			
Midnight			

Date			Day
Morning (Fasting)			
Before Lunch			
After Lunch			
Evening (Before dinner)			
Before Bed (after dinner)			
Midnight			

Date			Day
Morning (Fasting)			
Before Lunch			
After Lunch			
Evening (Before dinner)			
Before Bed (after dinner)			
Midnight			

Other information

Date		**Day**	
Time	Blood sugar (mg/dl)	Blood pressure (mmHg)	Insulin dose/Notes
Morning (Fasting)			
Before Lunch			
After Lunch			
Evening (Before dinner)			
Before Bed (after dinner)			
Midnight			

Date		**Day**	
Morning (Fasting)			
Before Lunch			
After Lunch			
Evening (Before dinner)			
Before Bed (after dinner)			
Midnight			

Date		**Day**	
Morning (Fasting)			
Before Lunch			
After Lunch			
Evening (Before dinner)			
Before Bed (after dinner)			
Midnight			

Other information

WEEKLY SUMMARY

Weekly readings Summary

Day	Fasting	Before lunch	After lunch	Evening before dinner	After dinner	Midnight	Blood pressure
Average							

Reflections on diet, exercise, and overall health

Any changes in medication or lifestyle

Goals for the next week

Date		**Day**	
Time	Blood sugar (mg/dl)	Blood pressure (mmHg)	Insulin dose/Notes
Morning (Fasting)			
Before Lunch			
After Lunch			
Evening (Before dinner)			
Before Bed (after dinner)			
Midnight			

Date		**Day**	
Morning (Fasting)			
Before Lunch			
After Lunch			
Evening (Before dinner)			
Before Bed (after dinner)			
Midnight			

Date		**Day**	
Morning (Fasting)			
Before Lunch			
After Lunch			
Evening (Before dinner)			
Before Bed (after dinner)			
Midnight			

Other information

Date		Day		
Time		Blood sugar (mg/dl)	Blood pressure (mmHg)	Insulin dose/Notes
Morning (Fasting)				
Before Lunch				
After Lunch				
Evening (Before dinner)				
Before Bed (after dinner)				
Midnight				

Date		Day		
Morning (Fasting)				
Before Lunch				
After Lunch				
Evening (Before dinner)				
Before Bed (after dinner)				
Midnight				

Date		Day		
Morning (Fasting)				
Before Lunch				
After Lunch				
Evening (Before dinner)				
Before Bed (after dinner)				
Midnight				

Other information

Date			Day
Time	Blood sugar (mg/dl)	Blood pressure (mmHg)	Insulin dose/Notes
Morning (Fasting)			
Before Lunch			
After Lunch			
Evening (Before dinner)			
Before Bed (after dinner)			
Midnight			

Date			Day
Morning (Fasting)			
Before Lunch			
After Lunch			
Evening (Before dinner)			
Before Bed (after dinner)			
Midnight			

Date			Day
Morning (Fasting)			
Before Lunch			
After Lunch			
Evening (Before dinner)			
Before Bed (after dinner)			
Midnight			

Other information

Weekly readings Summary

Day	Fasting	Before lunch	After lunch	Evening before dinner	After dinner	Midnight	Blood pressure
Average							

Reflections on diet, exercise, and overall health

Any changes in medication or lifestyle

Goals for the next week

Date			Day
Time	Blood sugar (mg/dl)	Blood pressure (mmHg)	Insulin dose/Notes
Morning (Fasting)			
Before Lunch			
After Lunch			
Evening (Before dinner)			
Before Bed (after dinner)			
Midnight			

Date			Day
Morning (Fasting)			
Before Lunch			
After Lunch			
Evening (Before dinner)			
Before Bed (after dinner)			
Midnight			

Date			Day
Morning (Fasting)			
Before Lunch			
After Lunch			
Evening (Before dinner)			
Before Bed (after dinner)			
Midnight			

Other information

Date		Day	
Time	Blood sugar (mg/dl)	Blood pressure (mmHg)	Insulin dose/Notes
Morning (Fasting)			
Before Lunch			
After Lunch			
Evening (Before dinner)			
Before Bed (after dinner)			
Midnight			

Date		Day	
Morning (Fasting)			
Before Lunch			
After Lunch			
Evening (Before dinner)			
Before Bed (after dinner)			
Midnight			

Date		Day	
Morning (Fasting)			
Before Lunch			
After Lunch			
Evening (Before dinner)			
Before Bed (after dinner)			
Midnight			

Other information

Date			Day
Time	Blood sugar (mg/dl)	Blood pressure (mmHg)	Insulin dose/Notes
Morning (Fasting)			
Before Lunch			
After Lunch			
Evening (Before dinner)			
Before Bed (after dinner)			
Midnight			

Date			Day
Morning (Fasting)			
Before Lunch			
After Lunch			
Evening (Before dinner)			
Before Bed (after dinner)			
Midnight			

Date			Day
Morning (Fasting)			
Before Lunch			
After Lunch			
Evening (Before dinner)			
Before Bed (after dinner)			
Midnight			

Other information

Weekly readings Summary

Day	Fasting	Before lunch	After lunch	Evening before dinner	After dinner	Midnight	Blood pressure
Average							

Reflections on diet, exercise, and overall health

Any changes in medication or lifestyle

Goals for the next week

Date			Day
Time	Blood sugar (mg/dl)	Blood pressure (mmHg)	Insulin dose/Notes
Morning (Fasting)			
Before Lunch			
After Lunch			
Evening (Before dinner)			
Before Bed (after dinner)			
Midnight			

Date			Day
Morning (Fasting)			
Before Lunch			
After Lunch			
Evening (Before dinner)			
Before Bed (after dinner)			
Midnight			

Date			Day
Morning (Fasting)			
Before Lunch			
After Lunch			
Evening (Before dinner)			
Before Bed (after dinner)			
Midnight			

Other information

Date			Day
Time	Blood sugar (mg/dl)	Blood pressure (mmHg)	Insulin dose/Notes
Morning (Fasting)			
Before Lunch			
After Lunch			
Evening (Before dinner)			
Before Bed (after dinner)			
Midnight			

Date			Day
Morning (Fasting)			
Before Lunch			
After Lunch			
Evening (Before dinner)			
Before Bed (after dinner)			
Midnight			

Date			Day
Morning (Fasting)			
Before Lunch			
After Lunch			
Evening (Before dinner)			
Before Bed (after dinner)			
Midnight			

Other information

Date		Day	
Time	Blood sugar (mg/dl)	Blood pressure (mmHg)	Insulin dose/Notes
Morning (Fasting)			
Before Lunch			
After Lunch			
Evening (Before dinner)			
Before Bed (after dinner)			
Midnight			

Date		Day	
Morning (Fasting)			
Before Lunch			
After Lunch			
Evening (Before dinner)			
Before Bed (after dinner)			
Midnight			

Date		Day	
Morning (Fasting)			
Before Lunch			
After Lunch			
Evening (Before dinner)			
Before Bed (after dinner)			
Midnight			

Other information

WEEKLY SUMMARY

Weekly readings Summary

Day	Fasting	Before lunch	After lunch	Evening before dinner	After dinner	Midnight	Blood pressure
Average							

Reflections on diet, exercise, and overall health

Any changes in medication or lifestyle

Goals for the next week

GRAPH SHOWING MONTHLY _________________ (FASTING/PRANDIAL) BLOOD GLUCOSE LEVEL TREND

Plot your blood glucose values on the graph and join the points

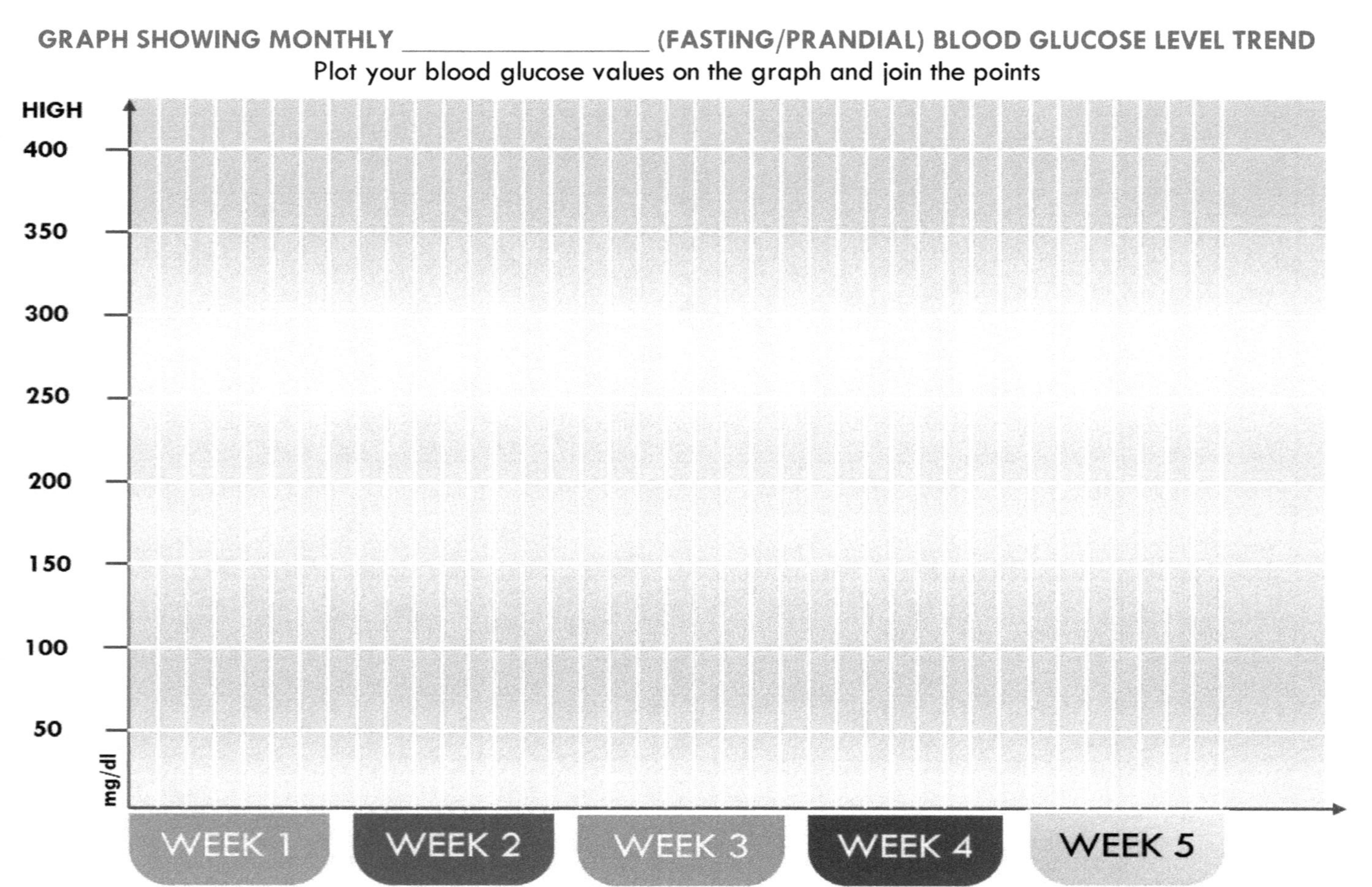

GRAPH SHOWING MONTHLY ________________ (FASTING/PRANDIAL) BLOOD GLUCOSE LEVEL TREND

Plot your blood glucose values on the graph and join the points

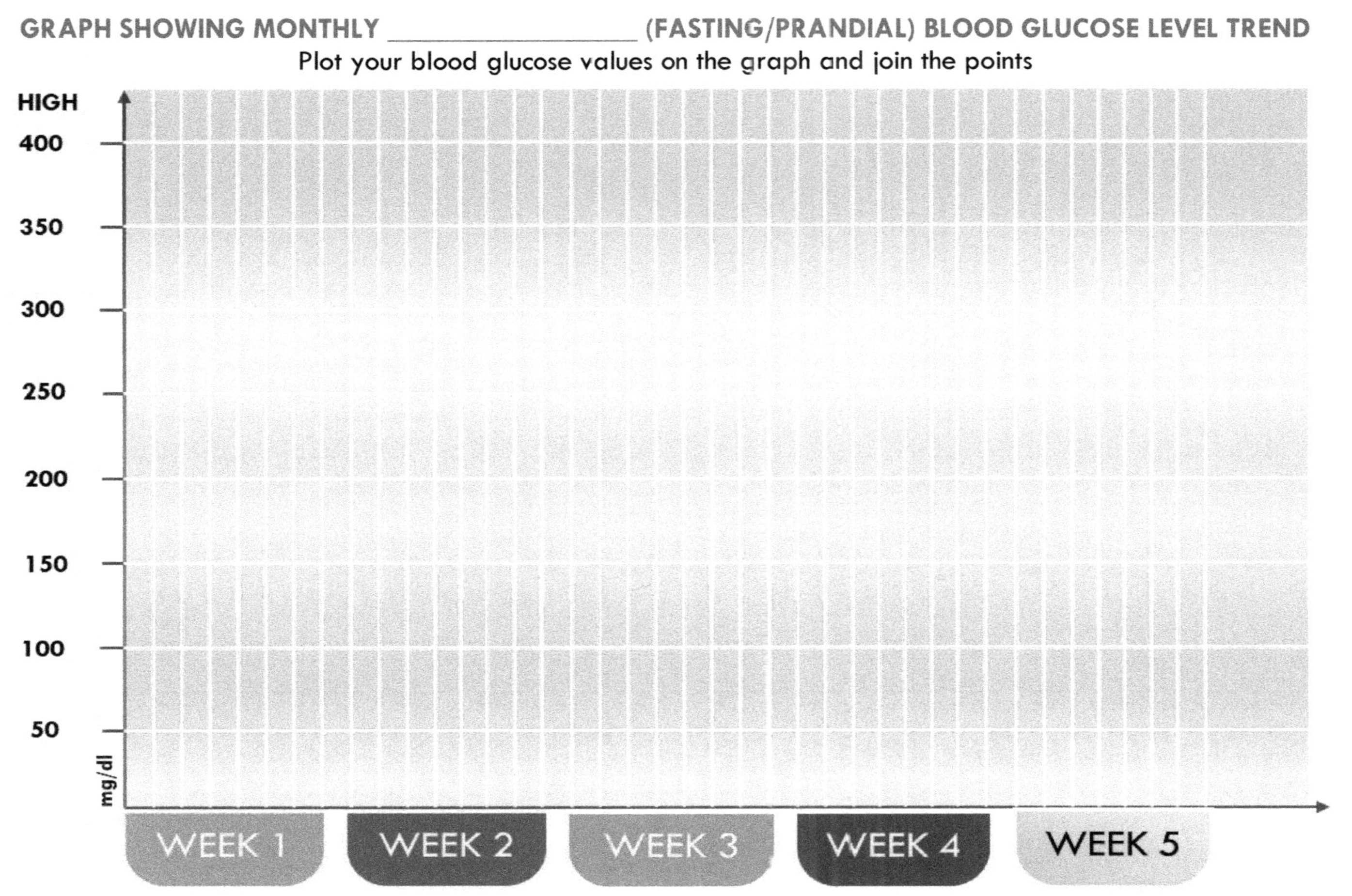

Reflections on diet, exercise, and overall health

Any changes in medication or lifestyle

Goals for the next month

Points to discuss with my doctor

GLYCEMIC GOALS FOR DIABETES MELLITUS

Parameter	AACE	IDF	ADA/RSSDI
HbA1c	≤6.5	≤6.5	<7
FBS	<110	<100	80-130
PPBS	<140	<160	<180

AACE – American academy of clinical endocrinology

IDF – International diabetic federation

ADA – American diabetic association

RSSDI - Research Society for the Study of Diabetes in India

Date			Day
Time	Blood sugar (mg/dl)	Blood pressure (mmHg)	Insulin dose/Notes
Morning (Fasting)			
Before Lunch			
After Lunch			
Evening (Before dinner)			
Before Bed (after dinner)			
Midnight			

Date			Day
Morning (Fasting)			
Before Lunch			
After Lunch			
Evening (Before dinner)			
Before Bed (after dinner)			
Midnight			

Date			Day
Morning (Fasting)			
Before Lunch			
After Lunch			
Evening (Before dinner)			
Before Bed (after dinner)			
Midnight			

Other information

Date			Day
Time	Blood sugar (mg/dl)	Blood pressure (mmHg)	Insulin dose/Notes
Morning (Fasting)			
Before Lunch			
After Lunch			
Evening (Before dinner)			
Before Bed (after dinner)			
Midnight			

Date			Day
Morning (Fasting)			
Before Lunch			
After Lunch			
Evening (Before dinner)			
Before Bed (after dinner)			
Midnight			

Date			Day
Morning (Fasting)			
Before Lunch			
After Lunch			
Evening (Before dinner)			
Before Bed (after dinner)			
Midnight			

Other information

Date			Day
Time	Blood sugar (mg/dl)	Blood pressure (mmHg)	Insulin dose/Notes
Morning (Fasting)			
Before Lunch			
After Lunch			
Evening (Before dinner)			
Before Bed (after dinner)			
Midnight			

Date			Day
Morning (Fasting)			
Before Lunch			
After Lunch			
Evening (Before dinner)			
Before Bed (after dinner)			
Midnight			

Date			Day
Morning (Fasting)			
Before Lunch			
After Lunch			
Evening (Before dinner)			
Before Bed (after dinner)			
Midnight			

Other information

Weekly readings Summary

Day	Fasting	Before lunch	After lunch	Evening before dinner	After dinner	Midnight	Blood pressure
Average							

Reflections on diet, exercise, and overall health

Any changes in medication or lifestyle

Goals for the next week

Date			Day
Time	Blood sugar (mg/dl)	Blood pressure (mmHg)	Insulin dose/Notes
Morning (Fasting)			
Before Lunch			
After Lunch			
Evening (Before dinner)			
Before Bed (after dinner)			
Midnight			

Date			Day
Morning (Fasting)			
Before Lunch			
After Lunch			
Evening (Before dinner)			
Before Bed (after dinner)			
Midnight			

Date			Day
Morning (Fasting)			
Before Lunch			
After Lunch			
Evening (Before dinner)			
Before Bed (after dinner)			
Midnight			

Other information

Date			Day
Time	Blood sugar (mg/dl)	Blood pressure (mmHg)	Insulin dose/Notes
Morning (Fasting)			
Before Lunch			
After Lunch			
Evening (Before dinner)			
Before Bed (after dinner)			
Midnight			

Date			Day
Morning (Fasting)			
Before Lunch			
After Lunch			
Evening (Before dinner)			
Before Bed (after dinner)			
Midnight			

Date			Day
Morning (Fasting)			
Before Lunch			
After Lunch			
Evening (Before dinner)			
Before Bed (after dinner)			
Midnight			

Other information

Date		Day	
Time	Blood sugar (mg/dl)	Blood pressure (mmHg)	Insulin dose/Notes
Morning (Fasting)			
Before Lunch			
After Lunch			
Evening (Before dinner)			
Before Bed (after dinner)			
Midnight			

Date		Day	
Morning (Fasting)			
Before Lunch			
After Lunch			
Evening (Before dinner)			
Before Bed (after dinner)			
Midnight			

Date		Day	
Morning (Fasting)			
Before Lunch			
After Lunch			
Evening (Before dinner)			
Before Bed (after dinner)			
Midnight			

Other information

Weekly readings Summary

Day	Fasting	Before lunch	After lunch	Evening before dinner	After dinner	Midnight	Blood pressure
Average							

Reflections on diet, exercise, and overall health

Any changes in medication or lifestyle

Goals for the next week

Date		**Day**	
Time	Blood sugar (mg/dl)	Blood pressure (mmHg)	Insulin dose/Notes
Morning (Fasting)			
Before Lunch			
After Lunch			
Evening (Before dinner)			
Before Bed (after dinner)			
Midnight			

Date		**Day**	
Morning (Fasting)			
Before Lunch			
After Lunch			
Evening (Before dinner)			
Before Bed (after dinner)			
Midnight			

Date		**Day**	
Morning (Fasting)			
Before Lunch			
After Lunch			
Evening (Before dinner)			
Before Bed (after dinner)			
Midnight			

Other information

Date			Day
Time	Blood sugar (mg/dl)	Blood pressure (mmHg)	Insulin dose/Notes
Morning (Fasting)			
Before Lunch			
After Lunch			
Evening (Before dinner)			
Before Bed (after dinner)			
Midnight			

Date			Day
Morning (Fasting)			
Before Lunch			
After Lunch			
Evening (Before dinner)			
Before Bed (after dinner)			
Midnight			

Date			Day
Morning (Fasting)			
Before Lunch			
After Lunch			
Evening (Before dinner)			
Before Bed (after dinner)			
Midnight			

Other information

Date		**Day**	
Time	Blood sugar (mg/dl)	Blood pressure (mmHg)	Insulin dose/Notes
Morning (Fasting)			
Before Lunch			
After Lunch			
Evening (Before dinner)			
Before Bed (after dinner)			
Midnight			

Date		**Day**	
Morning (Fasting)			
Before Lunch			
After Lunch			
Evening (Before dinner)			
Before Bed (after dinner)			
Midnight			

Date		**Day**	
Morning (Fasting)			
Before Lunch			
After Lunch			
Evening (Before dinner)			
Before Bed (after dinner)			
Midnight			

Other information

Weekly readings Summary

Day	Fasting	Before lunch	After lunch	Evening before dinner	After dinner	Midnight	Blood pressure
Average							

Reflections on diet, exercise, and overall health

Any changes in medication or lifestyle

Goals for the next week

Date		Day	
Time	Blood sugar (mg/dl)	Blood pressure (mmHg)	Insulin dose/Notes
Morning (Fasting)			
Before Lunch			
After Lunch			
Evening (Before dinner)			
Before Bed (after dinner)			
Midnight			

Date		Day	
Morning (Fasting)			
Before Lunch			
After Lunch			
Evening (Before dinner)			
Before Bed (after dinner)			
Midnight			

Date		Day	
Morning (Fasting)			
Before Lunch			
After Lunch			
Evening (Before dinner)			
Before Bed (after dinner)			
Midnight			

Other information

Date		Day	
Time	Blood sugar (mg/dl)	Blood pressure (mmHg)	Insulin dose/Notes
Morning (Fasting)			
Before Lunch			
After Lunch			
Evening (Before dinner)			
Before Bed (after dinner)			
Midnight			

Date		Day	
Morning (Fasting)			
Before Lunch			
After Lunch			
Evening (Before dinner)			
Before Bed (after dinner)			
Midnight			

Date		Day	
Morning (Fasting)			
Before Lunch			
After Lunch			
Evening (Before dinner)			
Before Bed (after dinner)			
Midnight			

Other information

Date		**Day**	
Time	Blood sugar (mg/dl)	Blood pressure (mmHg)	Insulin dose/Notes
Morning (Fasting)			
Before Lunch			
After Lunch			
Evening (Before dinner)			
Before Bed (after dinner)			
Midnight			

Date		**Day**	
Morning (Fasting)			
Before Lunch			
After Lunch			
Evening (Before dinner)			
Before Bed (after dinner)			
Midnight			

Date		**Day**	
Morning (Fasting)			
Before Lunch			
After Lunch			
Evening (Before dinner)			
Before Bed (after dinner)			
Midnight			

Other information

WEEKLY SUMMARY

Weekly readings Summary							
Day	Fasting	Before lunch	After lunch	Evening before dinner	After dinner	Midnight	Blood pressure
Average							

Reflections on diet, exercise, and overall health

Any changes in medication or lifestyle

Goals for the next week

MONTHLY SUMMARY

GRAPH SHOWING MONTHLY _____________________ (FASTING/PRANDIAL) BLOOD GLUCOSE LEVEL TREND

Plot your blood glucose values on the graph and join the points

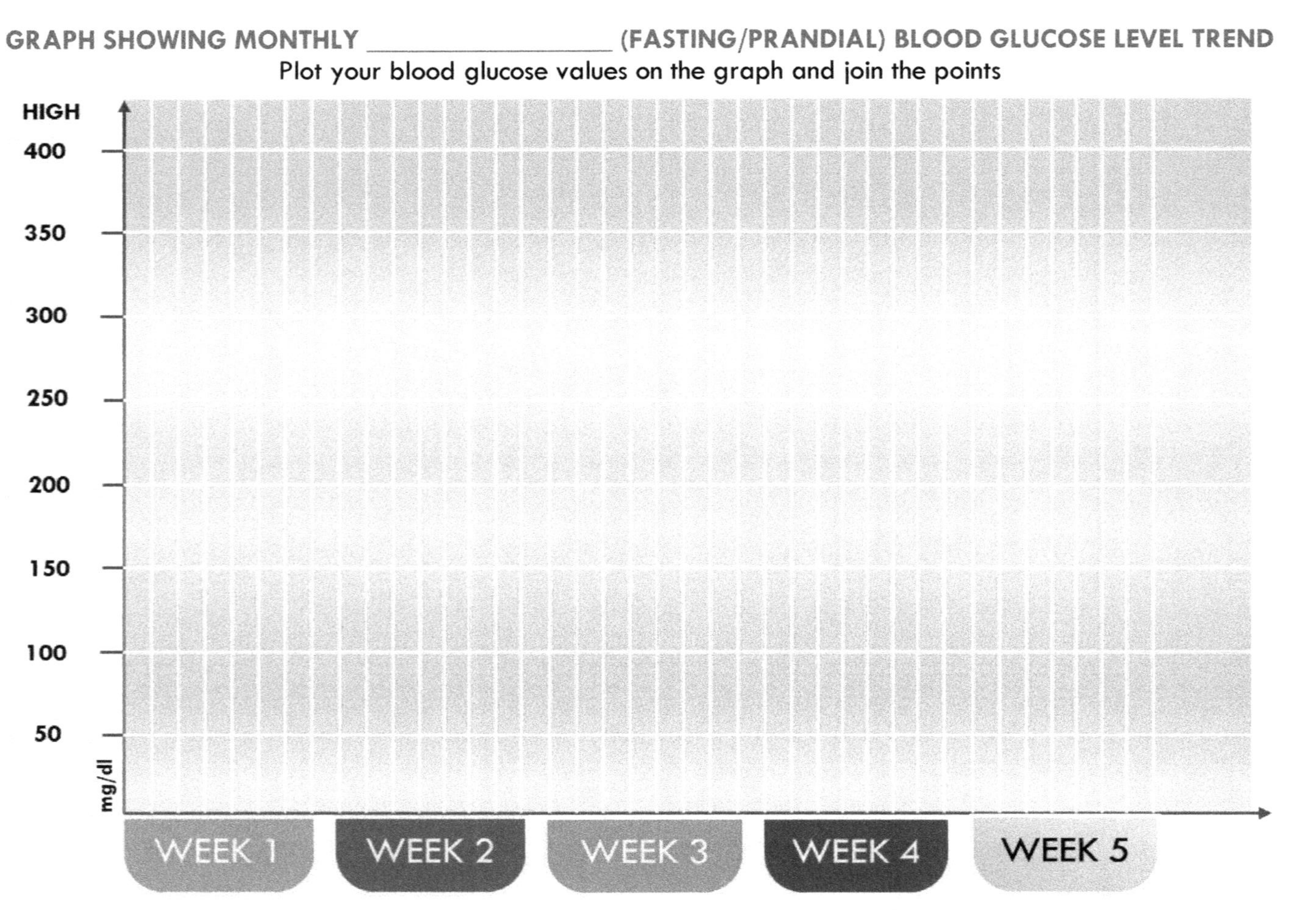

MONTHLY SUMMARY

GRAPH SHOWING MONTHLY _________________ (FASTING/PRANDIAL) BLOOD GLUCOSE LEVEL TREND

Plot your blood glucose values on the graph and join the points

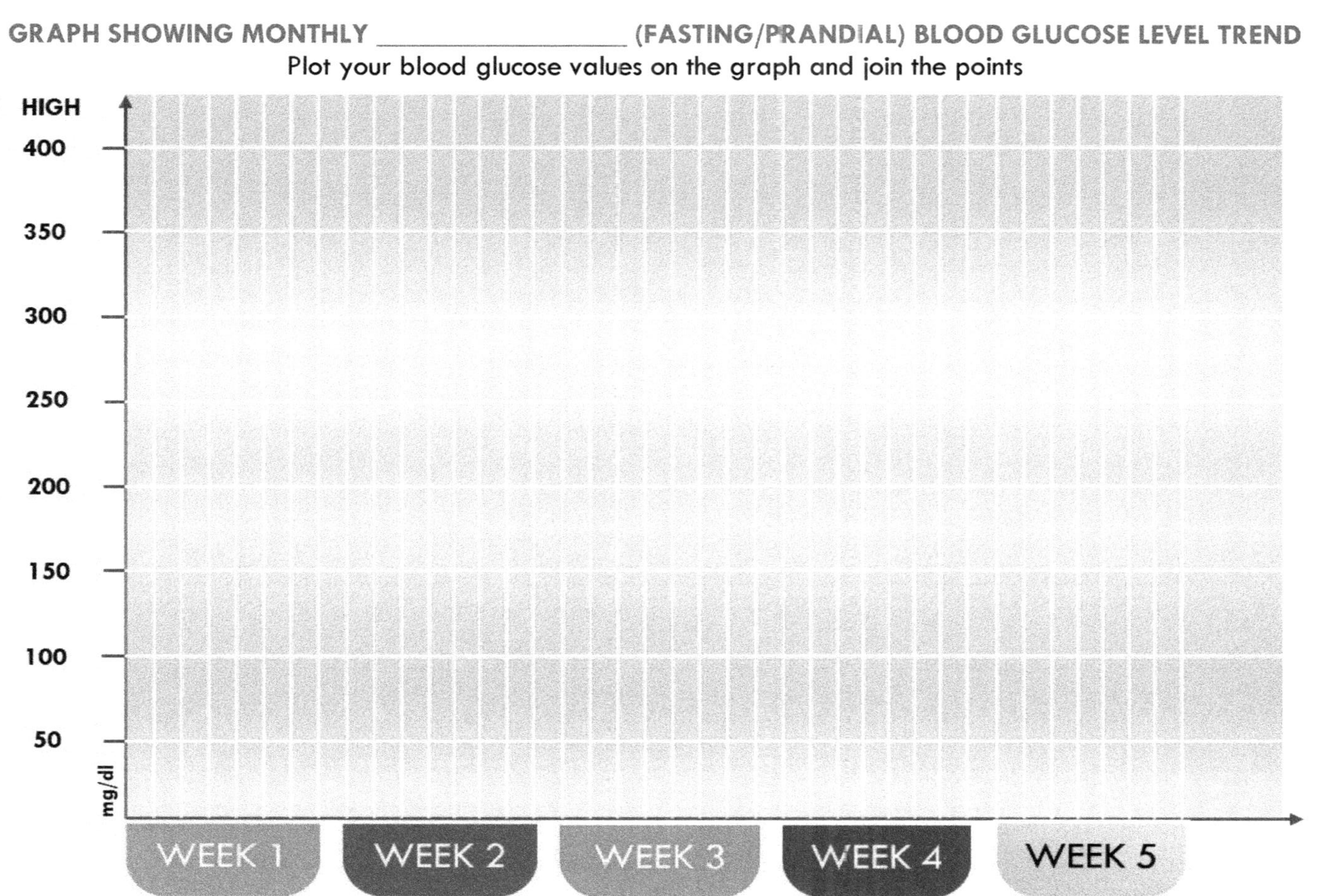

MONTHLY SUMMARY

Reflections on diet, exercise, and overall health

Any changes in medication or lifestyle

Goals for the next month

Points to discuss with my doctor

INSULIN INJECTION SITE & TECHNIQUE

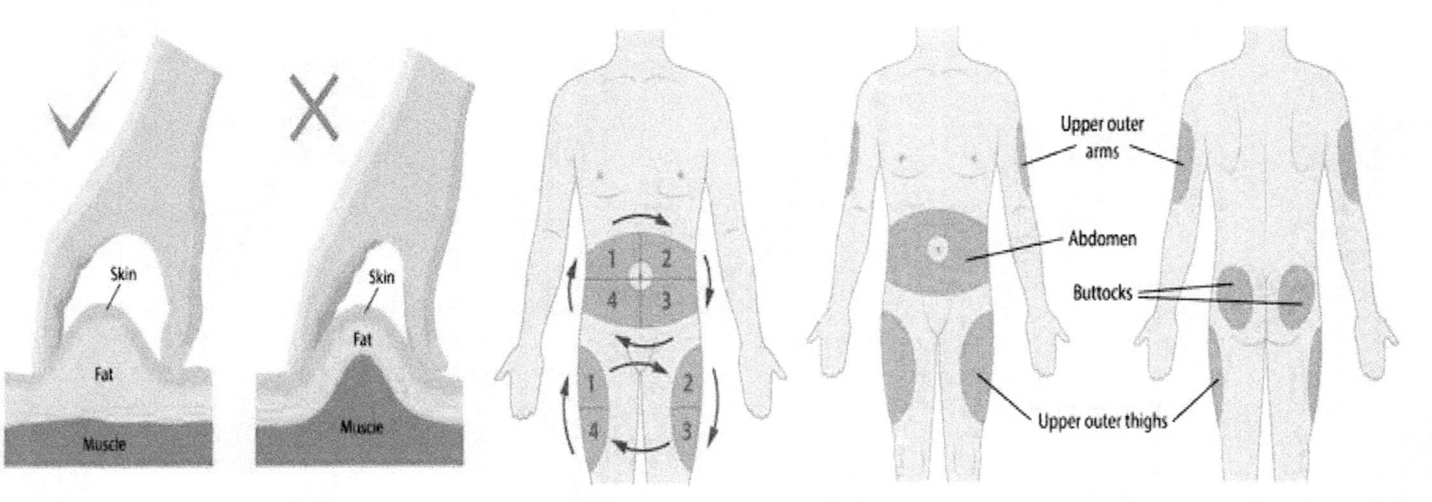

GUIDE FOR HOME MANAGEMENT OF HYPOGLYCEMIA

What is Hypoglycemia?
Hypoglycemia occurs when your blood sugar level drops below 70 mg/dL. It requires immediate attention to prevent serious complications.

Symptoms of Hypoglycemia
- Mild: Shakiness, sweating, dizziness, hunger, irritability, rapid heartbeat
- Moderate: Confusion, blurred vision, weakness, difficulty concentrating
- Severe: Inability to eat/drink, seizures, loss of consciousness

Immediate Steps to Manage Hypoglycemia

1. Check Blood Sugar - Use your glucometer to check if you have symptoms.

2. **Consume Fast-Acting Carbohydrates** - If below 70 mg/dL, consume 15 grams of fast-acting carbs:
   - 4 glucose tablets
   - 1 tube glucose gel
   - 1/2 cup (120 ml) regular soda (not diet)
   - 1 tablespoon sugar, honey, or corn syrup
   - 1 cup (240 ml) skim milk
   - 1/2 cup (120 ml) fruit juice
   - 5-6 pieces hard candy

3. **Recheck Blood Sugar** - Wait 15 minutes, then recheck your blood sugar level.

4. **Repeat if Necessary** - If still below 70 mg/dL, repeat the steps until it's above 70 mg/dL.

5. **Follow Up with a Snack** - Eat a small snack if your next meal is more than an hour away (e.g., peanut butter sandwich, cheese and crackers, yogurt and fruit).

6. **Preventing Future Episodes**
- Monitor Regularly: Check blood sugar levels as recommended.
- Eat Regularly: Do not skip meals; eat balanced meals with carbs, proteins, and fats.
- Carry Carbs: Always have glucose tablets, candy, or juice with you.
- Adjust Medications: Consult your healthcare provider if you have frequent hypoglycemia.
- Wear ID: Wear a medical alert bracelet or carry an ID card indicating diabetes.

> **When to Seek Medical Help**
> - Severe hypoglycemia (loss of consciousness, seizures) requires immediate medical attention.
> - Frequent episodes should be discussed with your healthcare provider to adjust your management plan

NOTES